MW00335407

CHEYENNE RISING SUN

TWO MEN A CENTURY APART SAW THE FUTURE

JOHN A. KURI

SEVEN LOCKS PRESS

Santa Ana, California

© 2004 by John A. Kuri. All rights reserved.

No part of this publication may be reproduced, distributed, or transmitted in any form or by any means, including photocopying, recording, or other electronic or mechanical methods, or by any information storage and retrieval system, without prior written permission from the publisher, except for brief quotations embodied in critical reviews and certain other noncommercial uses permitted by copyright law. For permission requests, write to the publisher, addressed "Attention: Permissions Coordinator," at the address below.

Seven Locks Press
P.O. Box 25689
Santa Ana, CA 92799
(800) 354-5348

Individual Sales. This book is available through most bookstores or can be ordered directly from Seven Locks Press at the address above.

Quantity Sales. Special discounts are available on quantity purchases by corporations, associations, and others. For details, contact the "Special Sales Department" at the publisher's address above.

Printed in the United States of America

Library of Congress Cataloging-in-Publication Data
is available from the publisher
ISBN 1-931643-46-6

Cover design by John Van Hamersveld

The author and publisher assume neither liability nor responsibility to any person or entity with respect to any direct or indirect loss or damage caused, or alleged to be caused, by the information contained herein, or for errors, omissions, inaccuracies, or any other inconsistency within these pages, or for unintentional slights against people or organizations.

DEDICATION

To:

Morning Star, whose legacy for all people stands taller with each passing decade;

And, to **Ted Rising Sun**. From where you view us now, thank you for never giving up on us mortals and, for the inspiration to look beyond ourselves to the future.

CONTENTS

ACKNOWLEDGEMENTS

The author wishes to acknowledge:

Doug Gorman, who, without hesitation, entrusted this coveted source of history to me;

Turah Miller, who came to the call, altruistically, making this effort possible;

Doreen Pond, who lived much of this—looked in my eyes, and then spoke from her heart;

Imogene Rising Sun, who understands more than anyone, Ted, and so willingly brought me into her private world;

Art McDonald, Ph.D., who with one subtle phrase, both as the sage he is, and as my compadre, guided me towards this journey that otherwise would never have been realized;

Fred Kuri, my brother, who through his own dedication and perseverance, inspired my first attempt at writing.

Jennifer White Kuri, my fulfilling half and eternal partner, whose spirit embraced this effort and whose encouragement was unwavering;

Paul Glass, who was instrumental in the publishing of the book *Cheyenne Journey*, and believed totally in this effort.

KaDo Gorman, for her assistance with the academic research phase, and for the major effort to proof the original manuscript.

Rita McDonald, who, as with all things, nurtured from the background.

Karyn Gorman, Ph.D, who so willingly shared her experience in Indian Health Care, giving me additional insight.

Jim Riordan and his staff at Seven Locks Press, for handling this work with so much care and expedience.

PREFACE

America has not always been unaware of certain shameful behavior. At the beginning of the nineteenth century, President Thomas Jefferson, when instructing Meriwether Lewis before the now famous expedition of 1804, said, "You serve the cause to bring honor to our character, as you will be sure to encounter many Indians. Word of the injuries we have done their brothers in our states must be known to them, and so a careful and respectful eye to their traditions is of paramount importance."

This honorable presidential sentiment was lost in the mid-century hunger for all the land west of the Mississippi. As millions of acres were swallowed by intruding Europeans immigrating west following the Louisiana Purchase, or by the Spaniards who had pushed north through Mexico during the eighteenth century actively pursuing the gold and silver of the mountains and feeding the Indian slave trade in Santa Fe with captured Indian women and children, this vast land that had been the home to numerous tribes, including the Northern Cheyenne, was forever changed along with the lives of its inhabitants.

As the long-fought Indian wars came to an end, the U.S. government set up the reservation system. The freedom of an

Indian lifestyle based on their traditional skills as hunters and gatherers was, by contract, substituted for a type of welfare dependency in which all the Indian people's needs were to be provided by the government in exchange for all the land that had once been theirs.

When considering the significance of this promise, one must think of the scale of the region west of the Mississippi and its natural resources. Millions of acres populated by vast herds of buffalo and other game, lakes and streams with bountiful varieties of fish, fertile soil that gave corn and other crops—this had been mother earth to the American Indian. To hand all of this over based on a contract with a government, laying down their weapons and ceasing their fight against encroachment, was a painful decision. Not only were centuries of a traditional lifestyle abandoned, the Indians' self-dependency was also surrendered to this promise from a government that had continually broken earlier treaties. All of the American Indians' food, water, medicine, education, and governance were in the hands of those who had taken their land.

Morning Star, the great Northern Cheyenne Chief, was the first to recognize that the Indian's world had permanently changed. To stop the bloodshed and look to the future, Morning Star agreed to turn over the welfare of his people to a reservation in Oklahoma, 750 miles south of their ancestral home. This was done with the pledge that if it did not suit them after the first year the Northern Cheyenne could return to their homeland. Most importantly, it was done with an eye towards the education of his people so that the children could learn the ways of the white man.

What was provided was not what had been promised. After the first year, Morning Star refused to let his people continue to die from malaria, cholera, and malnutrition at the hands of the U.S. government. Under the Chief's leadership, 350 Cheyenne walked north 750 miles, evading 12,000 pursuing U.S. cavalry, until they reached Fort Robinson, Nebraska. There, Morning Star lost almost a third of his remaining people to army gunfire before the government relented and granted the Cheyenne their own reservation, ironically on land that once was their own.

Almost 100 years later, Ted Rising Sun, the great grandson of Morning Star, with years of service in the U.S. Army, combat in North Korea, and numerous honors, returned to the reservation and realized it was his purpose in life to confront the government, as had Morning Star, and force them to honor their commitment to all Indians for real education for the children.

The events within this story occurred largely as written. The characters are real. The individuals depicted as Bureau of Indian Affairs officials have fictional names so as to protect their identity. However, this writing accurately depicts the twentieth century events that occurred in both Lame Deer, Montana, and Washington, D.C., with the Bureau of Indian Affairs, and the little-known nineteenth century story of Morning Star and his people's escape from what certainly would have been extinction.

The letter on the following page from the Morning Star Memorial Foundation signed by Arthur McDonald, Ph.D., speaks to the validity of this writing *and offers an endorsement from a prominent American Indian who had the*

Morning Star

MEMORIAL FOUNDATION

John A. Kuri
Kuri Productions, Inc

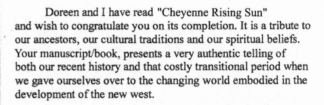

Re: "Cheyenne Rising Sun"

Dear John:

Doreen and I have read "Cheyenne Rising Sun" and wish to congratulate you on its completion. It is a tribute to our ancestors, our cultural traditions and our spiritual beliefs. Your manuscript/book, presents a very authentic telling of both our recent history and that costly transitional period when we gave ourselves over to the changing world embodied in the development of the new west.

When we first allowed you access to the Foundation's archived oral and written histories, we never imagined the project would include our important recent history. Our early conversations had been focused on the Fort Robinson Outbreak and the events leading up to that point. However, the parallels you have drawn between the lives and accomplishments of Morning Star and his grandson Ted Rising Sun are poignant and totally appropriate.

A few years prior to his passing, The National Indian Education Association honored Ted as the Indian Education Elder of The Year. At the awards ceremony, a Crow Elder came forward and sang an Honor song for Ted, a Northern Cheyenne. That was unprecedented! The novel you have written captures much of the importance of the lives of the two Cheyennes, Morning Star and Ted Rising Sun. We feel that this effort may be the best effort to date to accurately portray an important facet of the American Indian history which has been done so poorly by others.

We look forward to assisting you in any way needed as the project progresses.

Sincerely,

Arthur L. McDonald- Ph.D.

BUILDING SUCCESS
ON THE TRADITION
OF OUR PEOPLE

privilege of working with Ted Rising Sun. Therefore, what follows is a little background on Dr. McDonald and his associate at the Foundation, Doreen Pond. They were two critical sources of information during my research and then in the review of the finished manuscript.

Dr. McDonald, with his broad background in Indian Health and Education issues, and Doreen with her direct experience on the Northern Cheyenne Tribal Council and her years in Indian Education, offered immeasurable guidance.

Arthur L. "Paints Many Horses" McDonald, Ph.D., is an enrolled member of the Oglala Sioux tribe. He has served as the CEO of the Morning Star Memorial Foundation and was a Director of the Foundation for some years. He is a member of the American Psychological Association.

Dr. McDonald was the second American Indian to earn a Ph. D. in Psychology. His specific studies were in Human Factors Psychology at the University of South Dakota. He has been involved in Indian Health Care for years.

Dr. McDonald has coauthored numerous articles for publication in *Psychopharmacologia,* and *Journal of Psychology*, to name a few. He has written several reports, including "Definition of Indian Education," prepared for the American Indian Policy Review Commission, 1975. He has coauthored two books, including *Psychology and Contemporary Problems* (Brooks-Cole, 1974). He authored the chapter "Value Conflicts: A Reason for Indian Dropouts" in *The Schooling of Native America*, (Washington: Teachers Corp., 1978) and "The Northern Cheyenne Outbreak of 1879: Using oral history and archaeology as tools of resistance. In McGuire, R., Paynter, R. (Eds.) *The Archaeology of Inequality*, Oxford, UK: Blackwell.

The American Psychological Association honored Dr. McDonald in 1996 with the Lifetime Achievement Award in Training of Mental Health. He received the American Psychological Association Presidential Citation for Contributions to Psychological Services to American Indians and Alaska Natives in 2000, was honored with the "Keeper of the Fire" Award for Lifetime Dedication to Native American Indian Health Training in 2001, and was honored by the conference of the National Association of Rural Mental Health receiving the "Howry" Award.

Doreen "Walking Woman" Pond is an enrolled member of the Northern Cheyenne tribe. She was the second woman ever to serve on the Cheyenne Tribal Council (serving first as Ted Rising Sun's protégé followed by three separate terms). She was a Director of Development for the Morning Star Memorial Foundation and a member of the Board.

Ms. Pond received her B.A. in Administration and Community Development from Antioch College. She was involved with the Dull Knife Memorial College since its inception in 1973 and served as Dean of Business Affairs, Director of Institutional Development, and Vice President for Business Affairs. She is currently the supervisor of medical records for Indian Health Services Hospital in Phoenix, Arizona.

(Doreen was present, as a member of the Tribal Council, in the scenes depicted in that chamber within this writing. She also was present for much of what I write of the BIA meetings and conflicts. Doreen's late husband, Leland, was the attorney who handled the BIA matters covered within the manuscript. Their son, James, now a prominent member of the medical profession, wrote the poem that begins the Introduction.)

INTRODUCTION

I wince at the sound of my name
and hold the tears from my face
At times I want to hang my head in shame
all because of feelings toward my race.

I lose sleep at night
never wanting to be alone
Constantly wondering what's right
although racism is one thing I'll never condone.

I have large dreams of fortune and fame
which may never come true
There are several to blame for the bitterness,
but least of all you.

It is a silent fight
forever monotone
A wrong which will never be right
until the pain is sewn.

—James Pond

He knew not to breathe or move, even a finger.

The temptation was almost overwhelming. It was out there and that was why they must be quiet. Only ten years of age, Ted knew that if the creature sensed anything unusual, their location would be exposed. And that would be his fault. He would be shamed in the shadow of his father.

Ted strained his eyes so he might watch his father, Oliver, a man who was the final authority on all things in life. His head was locked into the natural cradle made from his right hand and wrist as he gripped the stock of the old 30/30 caliber Winchester.

"How big was it?" Ted pondered. He wished he could follow the line of sight delivered down the rifle barrel to his father's piercing eye. If only he could see what image his father was locked on. Then Ted would know.

In an instant, something changed. Ted sensed the moment had come. Perhaps it was the slight tightening of Oliver's grip on the rifle or that he had stopped breathing. The moment had become so still that Ted could hear the blood pumping within his own ears.

The sudden kick, roar, and burst of gun smoke stopped everything as the rifle fired. In what seemed to be slow motion, Ted watched as Oliver placed the rifle butt on the ground by his knee without breaking his sight of the shot. After a moment, he looked down at Ted.

"Want to see?"

"Can I?" Ted pleaded.

Oliver nodded and motioned for Ted to step in. Without hesitation the boy moved to his dad's side. Oliver pointed with his left arm and guided Ted's head with his right hand so the boy would know where to look.

Oliver was five-feet-ten-inches and well defined at 170 pounds. Dark hair, eyes, and dark skin, he was Cheyenne. His hands were strong, well worn, but in that moment, gentle. Oliver's noble face came from his grandfather, Morning Star, the great Cheyenne Chief.

Ted had all his dad's features but was too young to realize he also carried the same proud traditions of life passed down from Morning Star. Oliver often said to Ted, "You are Cheyenne." But with all the spiritual gifts of their traditional way of life came the burden of being an Indian trying to survive in a white man's world.

It was 1935 and more than fifty years since the last Cheyenne peace treaty with the government and army had been signed. Even with those years bridging time, Ted was not to forget that he would travel a different road than his white neighbors. Even though they lived in the same country and honored the same flag, nothing else was to be the same.

The buck was a six pointer. One clean shot had dropped him within two final steps. Ted stood a few feet back, watching as Oliver quickly opened the buck with his well-honed knife, the animal's steaming insides sliding onto the cold ground. To Ted, the buck seemed to be watching from those large black eyes. Within a few seconds, Oliver had retrieved the liver. He held it in the palm of his hand, steam rising in the brisk afternoon air. He cut a small piece from the deep red meat and raised it to his mouth with the blade of his knife. Ted watched as he ate the meat. Then Oliver offered the same to Ted.

"We honor the gift of our fallen brother. He has given his life so we may continue with ours, son."

And with those words Ted tasted the life passing from one creature of the earth to another. Without reluctance he accepted the gesture and seemed to understand the importance of the ritual. Most of the time Ted was more adult than child. Learning much of the Cheyenne spiritual tradition at his young age was not uncommon. Being the great grandson of the famed Chief, Morning Star, was. Ted's father, mother, and especially his grandmother, who was Morning Star's daughter, had all told him so often that grandmother earth and all her creatures were a gift from the Great Mystery, *Maheo*, the spiritual God of the Cheyenne. That was the way it had always been and the way it must be.

Grandmother had often spoken to the family about one of the great Cheyenne Chiefs who foretold a new order of things.

Once, only Indians lived in this land. Then came strangers from across the Great Water. No land had they; we gave them our land. No food had they; we gave them of our corn. The strangers are becoming many and they fill all the country. They dig gold from my mountains; they build houses of the trees of my forests; they rear cities of my stones and rocks; they make fine garments from the hides of animals that eat my grass. None of the things that make their riches did they bring with them from beyond the Great Water; all comes from my land, the land the Great Mystery gave unto the Indian.

And when I think upon this, I know that it is right, even this. In the heart of the Great Mystery it was meant that strangers/vistors—my friends across the Great Water—should come to my land; that I should bid them welcome; that all men should sit down with me and eat together of my corn. It was meant by the Great Mystery that the Indian should give to all people.

At ten, Ted believed his grandmother when she insisted that someday he would be the one to teach the Cheyenne way to others. This, because she knew, "They will want to learn."

Growing up in Busby and Lame Deer, Montana, today is hard. In Ted's beginning, it was rough. There was no electricity in the home. No plumbing, either. During winter, going to the bathroom meant a walk outside to the frozen outhouse. Night light came from coal-oil or candles. Going to school meant boarding in a Bureau of Indian Affairs (BIA) school. This was not an adventure, it was a systematic strangulation of a heritage and its traditions. School meant adopting white culture and eradicating the Cheyenne legacy.

At ten, how would Ted know that only six years into the future he would leave the area and find his way to a Mennonite high school in South Dakota? Attempting to enroll as a senior, he would be discouraged to learn that he could not even meet the qualifications for admission as a freshman. Despite his years in a BIA school, he simply had not been taught much that was useful.

Not even a teen yet, how would Ted know that he would one day find acceptance in the U.S. Army, be highly decorated while fighting a war in North Korea, but return to his homeland only to walk directly into the face of prejudice and bigotry? These obstacles to life and success would consume much of his adult days. They are not the unusual for the American Indian. They are the norm for the people who first occupied the land we take for granted as the United States.

Authors and pundits have asked: What is it to be an American? It is a considerable question because we are such a rich people with such diversification of culture coming together under one flag. But to understand that question from the perspective of the original people who inhabited this land, one must understand, to some degree, their legacy.

Many times I have heard the phrase, "Life is hard, and then you die." True, within a limited framework. For some, that is enough to breed mediocrity. Why bother to strive for anything better in life?

Ted's great grandfather, Morning Star, refused to dwell on the injustice his people suffered. Rather, he looked to the future and insisted that survival meant adapting to whatever life brings. To Morning Star, school meant education. Education meant being competitive and productive. Ted believed in the wisdom of the great Cheyenne Chief. This essential confidence gave Ted the strength to overcome not only the cultural barriers but his own self-inflicted pain. In doing this, he achieved something great for his people. Like his great grandfather, Ted was to rise above the adversity born from his place in life and once again prove that the clear vision of one true voice can defy both the odds and the naysayers who would otherwise have one exist in a paralysis that grips their culture as it is surrounded by a changing world.

And now you will read Ted's story. I promise you this: His story is not a fantasy from the world of Hollywood where one generally finds quixotic heroes of action achieving unrealistic feats that have been motivated by the need to defeat some contrived villain. Ted's enemies, both external and internal, were real, as are our own.

CHAPTER 1
SAND CREEK

Once the horizon in this part of the country is witnessed, only then will you truly embrace the term "Big Sky." On this particular afternoon, brush strokes of cumulus clouds seemed to bring that vast eternal blue closer to the warm prairie landscape. But the view was split in half by a black ribbon of asphalt. As I think about it, a highway cutting through all that beautiful open space is incongruous with the essence of the picture. However, it more or less defines our culture. Roadways give birth to transportation that gives birth to expansion and in turn that becomes some measure of progress. Now let's get back to the landscape.

Some years the southeastern part of Colorado is blanketed by black-eyed Susans. If you have never seen them, they are daisy-like wildflowers that typically line the country roads. In some valleys, the afternoon sun casts a warm luminosity on all those golden petals and they shimmer as one would only expect to see in fairy-tale inspired dreams. This land, however, was not only the fable rich edge to the frontier, it was and is the keeper of truth. For not all published history is unprejudiced. Mother earth, with her unvarnished memory, knows what the passing of each sun and moon has brought her, and by whose hand.

It was October, 1954. A mud-splattered '48 Ford pickup truck rolled down that highway. Ted "High Hawk" Rising Sun was riding in the truck bed and could just make out the newscast from the truck radio as the lone driver negotiated the road.

"President Eisenhower visited Fort Polk, Louisiana, today, welcoming home the 101st Airborne. With the Korean War over, life is getting back to normal for all our boys returning home to their families, loved ones, and jobs. . . . "

Ted looked off towards the open field. They were passing miles of untouched land with fence post after fence post strobing by. Something in that lonely view seemed to motivate his reach into the duffel bag. With precision, he plucked out a pint of whiskey, unscrewed the cap with some thought, then took a good, satisfying pull.

"How many miles of fencing in this part of the country?" he wondered. "It wasn't that long ago there was none."

Ted looked to the driver and tapped the bottle's neck against the rear window. The man looked through the rearview mirror. Ted offered a drink but the driver declined, not that it didn't look good on this dry afternoon.

Ted turned back to the passing view. He lit a Camel with his Zippo, the trusted torch of the day. It was a well-worn, essential item. He liked the feel in his hands. It proudly displayed the U.S. Army emblem along with an inscription, "High Hawk." He took another good pull from the bottle.

Ted, with his ruddy complexion, black hair, and dark eyes, and in his short-sleeved shirt, looked like a hard man. On closer scrutiny, something else came through from his demeanor. He had a hungry, unsettled look. He was a hunter with no game in sight.

The Ford was rolling down that narrow country highway, aimed towards the Rockies. That sublime sight is something only seen east of those imposing mountains where they erupt from the floor of the great plains.

The truck approached a wide shoulder area and came to a stop under a big shade tree. The driver slapped the side of the door, making a hollow drum-like sound. Ted grabbed his bag and climbed out, bottle in one hand, duffel in the other.

"Thanks, buddy."

The driver acknowledged him with a slight gesture and then drove off. Ted watched as the truck continued down a dirt road on the other side of the highway, kicking up a dust cloud that reminded him how dry an afternoon it was. He took another pull of the whiskey. As he did, the glare from the sky overcame him. With closed eyes, he staggered a little before finding his footing.

He heard an approaching car and quickly offered his thumb. It was a new model convertible and had that nice smooth V-8 sound. The car blew on past and Ted watched as it disappeared over a slight incline. "Someday," he mused.

On a hot day, standing in the sun long enough, it will deceptively begin to feel cool. That is until something cold touches the skin. As Ted took another pull from the bottle, a little of that sweet whiskey dripped on his neck. As he wiped it, he realized how warm he was. In that instant, the shady spot under the big tree became irresistible.

Leaning against that old tree, Ted felt comfortable, and perhaps isolated enough to relax. He looked up at its layers of branches and thought about how much had passed by that spot within view of that majestic tree.

Ted took another drink. The bottle was near empty as he sat it down beside him. His gaze took in what lay before him. More of that open space that offered a natural grazing land. It rose from an almost dry wash just in front of him to a slight ridge fifty yards away. Ted's eyes fell on some person's discarded pile of debris made up of a few pieces of sun-aged lumber and chunks of broken concrete, along with some paper cups and plates. The litter cluttered the otherwise undisturbed view and was another sign of the culture Ted was trying to understand.

The hot glare from the afternoon sky and golden field was so intense Ted closed his eyes. This was one of those moments when the eyelids are, oh, so heavy. Add to that the slight breeze and warm air, and anyone would be lulled to sleep. However, for Ted, this was to be much more. This was another of those moments when he would listen to the voice within his thoughts, the voice of his grandmother.

Her spirit had been his constant companion through North Korea. In fact, she had been with him since he first left home from Lame Deer, Montana, as a sixteen-year-old.

Slowly, deliberately, he could hear her voice. "Listen to me. Hear the story of our people."

A flutter in the debris caught Ted's attention, bringing him back to reality. It was a sparrow picking around the debris, searching for a meal. The bird was industrious as it cast about for food.

Grandmother continued to speak to Ted as he watched the bird. "The circle of life begins in the spring. That was when I was born, at the time the white men were coming."

After a few moments, the sparrow looked at Ted, as if to study him. Suddenly, the heavy sound of approaching horses broke the stillness and the sparrow, sensing jeopardy, flew off.

Ted looked towards the sound as it was intensifying. It came from the ridge line. Ted wanted to get to his feet but his body was so heavy he could not overcome the gravity he felt in that moment.

Grandmother's voice was persistent. "The Cheyenne people lived on these lands for hundreds of years."

Then to Ted's disbelief, he saw a flank of U.S. Cavalry slowly come into view on the ridge. In all, 700 men, many on horseback, appeared in every direction. The horses, eager for action, were difficult for their riders to contain. An ominous display of power was evident when four twelve-pounder mountain howitzers were rolled into view. The artillery soldiers began lining up the cannons and setting aim in Ted's direction.

Ted looked on in amazement. "Where am I? What the hell is going on?"

He could see both foot soldiers as well as cavalry forming what seemed to be a noose around the entire area. "Where did they come from?"

As Ted turned to look back to the highway, he saw an encampment of Indians. Three hundred Cheyenne and Arapaho, mostly women, children, and old men, were reacting to the approaching military threat. Panic was breaking out as the women gathered their young.

In the center of the encampment was the lodge of Black Kettle, the Cheyenne Chief. He stood calmly under an American flag that was tied atop a lodge pole held in his hand. The flag clearly fluttered in the afternoon breeze.

With a steady voice, the Chief called out in Cheyenne dialect, "Have no fear of the Blue Coats. I have made peace with their great leader." For indeed, Black Kettle had encamped exactly where the nearby military commander had instructed him to. Ted watched as Black Kettle motioned for his people to gather round him, under the cover of the U.S. flag.

On the edge of the encampment, Ted could see the foot soldiers running in, taking position with aimed rifles. Then he turned as the commander appeared in the center of the column. Colonel John Chivington, a large barrel-chested, severe-looking, bearded officer, was observing from the saddle. The horse mounted colors of the U.S. and the 3rd Colorado Regiment flew behind him.

On the colonel's right was Major Scott Anthony, a short and red-eyed officer whose face was swollen and pock-marked. The eyes were not red from the dust. This condition was the result of scurvy. All this added to his contemptible, Napoleonic air. In that same moment, three proud young officers on horseback approached the colonel. They wore their uniforms with a clear degree of self-esteem. Thirty-year-old Captain Silas Soule led, accompanied by two younger officers, Lieutenant Joseph Cramer, and Lieutenant James Connor.

Soule was so wrought, he almost screamed. "Sir, an attack would violate the pledge of safety given these people."

Chivington was enraged as he listened to these words.

Soule continued. "This will be murder in every sense of the word and will dishonor the uniform of the Army."

Chivington barked back, "Damn you, Captain Soule, and damn any man who sympathizes with Indians. I have come to kill *Indians*, and believe it is right and honorable to use any means under God's heaven to kill *Indians*. You will fall in rank, and you will attack at my command, or you will surely face a court-martial, the result of which shall see you face a firing squad."

Those chilling words, every syllable carrying considerable weight and meaning, raised the specter of doubt for the young officers. Soule and his men exchanged dubious glances.

Impatiently, Chivington continued, "Is that quite understood? Or do I have you three arrested here and now?"

The chain of command in the military is difficult to appreciate unless you have served. It is the very core by which authority is imposed on the many, in the face of extreme conditions. Field command in battle depends on it. Soule and his compatriots had suddenly realized that a military court would not look kindly on the actions of three junior, less experienced officers. After all, in the cold light of some distant courtroom, this act of disagreement would probably be mutiny.

Soule, now in respect to the uniform before him, responded with a quick, "Yes, sir."

Chivington, more concerned with the action in front of him, dismissed the men. "Return to your duties."

Soule wheeled his horse, and was followed immediately by Cramer and Connor.

As the men rode off, Chivington turned to Anthony, offering his prophecy. "Today, this field will *wade* in gore."

Anthony was gazing out at the frightened villagers. He was a man so disenchanted by his own misery that he seemed only capable of inflicting pain on others. He was slow to respond to Chivington. When he did, it was with some pleasure as he added, "And scalps."

Chivington offered his first battle instruction to Anthony. "Order B company to close in. Cut the Indians off from their ponies. I want *none* to escape!"

Ted was participating in a living nightmare. Hopelessly, he watched as the infantry moved up both ends of the creek, cutting off any possible escape.

White Antelope, the oldest of the Cheyenne Chiefs in the village, saw the approaching infantry and ran towards Chivington and Anthony's position, waving his arms. Edmond Guerrier, a young half-breed, tried to stop White Antelope, to no avail. The old man kept moving towards Chivington, wrestling himself free of Guerrier.

Chivington, from his perch atop his mount, watched a desperate White Antelope as he ran closer, pleading with the soldiers.

Chivington turned to a flank of infantry and raised his arm. "Marksmen! Take aim."

The men sighted their long rifles on the old man, who was running without a weapon, calling out in very clear English.

"STOP! STOP! STOP! We are here in peace." White Antelope continued to plead in all directions.

With certain pleasure, Chivington watched the frightened people. After a long moment, he completed the death sentence with the command, "FIRE!"

The marksmen opened fire, and the volley of shots took down White Antelope. This was immediately followed by the salvo of cannon fire. Their loads tore into the peaceful village, raining down hell on women, children, and the few men.

Ted was paralyzed by the horror of this unthinkable event. Unable to move, he remained a prisoner to this draconian experience. His grandmother had spoken of it so many times but now he was living it, seeing it with his own eyes.

In a valorous and extraordinary attempt at defense that was predictable from these most honorable of people, the thirty-five men of the Cheyenne village grabbed their few weapons to hastily form a perimeter around their loved ones. The women and children had huddled under the American flag, still flying in the hands of the trusted Chief, Black Kettle.

But rifle shots immediately followed the showering terror of the howitzers as teepees exploded, bodies fell, and blood colored the ground, forever leaving this act to the memory of the earth. The infantry and cavalry followed with an attack that had the fury of the Four Horsemen of the Apocalypse. Amidst flying lead, followed by bayonets, sabers, and lances, the military cut through the thin perimeter of protection leveling the brave Indian defense. Cheyenne and Arapaho scattered. Guerrier and Black Kettle were among the select few who managed to escape.

As unbelievable as it was to the youthful eyes of Soule, Crammer, and Connor, soldiers began slaughtering the women and children. No body was left with a scalp. A pregnant woman was slain, cut open, the infant removed, and then scalped.

Ted, now in a semi-delirious sweat, heard his grandmother as she began a chant in Cheyenne. "Nothing lives long, only the earth and the mountains."

Grandmother continued with her words to Ted. "Listen to me. Someday, they will want to know."

A man's voice suddenly shattered the moment. "Hey, Tonto. Wake up!"

The County Sheriff stepped up to Ted, giving him a little nudge with the toe of his boot. Ted looked up to see the Sheriff, who held Ted's discarded liquor bottle. This man looked like the law, his hand resting on the butt of his holstered revolver, eyes hidden behind dark aviator glasses.

"Whatta you doin', boy, littering my countryside with your empties?" the law inquired.

Ted did not respond.

"Better come with me."

Ted knew better than to resist. The officer cuffed Ted and walked him to his highway cruiser. As Ted moved to the car, he looked around at all the serenity. Then he realized that the devastation of moments ago was a memory never to be forgotten by the earth.

As the Sheriff closed the rear door, Ted was still consumed by his thoughts. Grandmother's voice continued again. "The massacre at Sand Creek was one of many broken promises. Morning Star, my father, your great grandfather, was the Cheyenne Chief who led us here, to our home in Montana. He knew our way of life was to be no more."

As the Sheriff pulled onto the roadway, Ted saw an historical road marker that read: *Colorado State Historical Marker. November 29, 1864. Site of The Sand Creek Massacre.*

One hundred fifty Cheyenne men, women, and children, under the protection of the American flag, were slaughtered and their corpses grotesquely mutilated in a massacre that shocked the nation.

Ted had heard this story so many times but somehow now it had become reality. What had drawn him to that spot at that moment? It had to have been coincidence. But was it?

Grandmother's voice would not stop. "The great white father in Washington promised Morning Star peace and a good place to live if we would stop the fighting."

The steel door slammed shut behind Ted. The officer turned the lock and then looked up. "You'll see the judge in the morning." The lawman moved down the corridor and disappeared through a door.

Ted moved a step away from the door and looked around the cell. A toilet, two beds, stone walls and floor, and that very cold steel. There were four other cells, all empty.

Ted sat on the lower bunk. The last of the day's sunlight found him, offering only a suggestion of warmth. As it quickly moved away, Ted laid back. His eyes went to the window where the sounds of life filtered through from the street at the end of an alley. After a moment, his eyes began to close. It was not but a few seconds later that he was asleep. To him, it was only a moment later that he awoke to the sound of a trustee offering him a plate of food.

"Hey, Chief. You want dinner?" the thin redneck sputtered.

Ted slowly focused as he looked up at the lone ceiling light. It was dark outside.

"Food. You want some food?" the trustee asked.

Ted got up and stepped over to grab his dinner, consisting of a plate of beans, white bread, and a cup of coffee. He said nothing as he took the meal and walked back to the bunk. He sat down and began eating. Ted was pretty damn hungry so he gave no thought to the taste of it. As he ate, he became even more tired than before and wondered if the jail cooks had put something in the meal, some kind of tranquilizer that kept inmates sedated.

Half finished, Ted laid back again and dropped into a deep sleep. He could have slept for days. Perhaps it was his mind's way of dealing with being locked up inside a stone and steel cage. But somewhere, in the haze of his sleep, he heard her voice. "You BASTARD!" she yelled.

Ted tossed and struggled in his sleep. His mind was plaguing him with a painful memory of his drunk wife as she pulled his two crying girls, one four, one six, away from Ted. "I'll never let you have these girls. Never. NEVER!"

Ted mumbled, "You don't know what you're saying. You're drunk."

The girls were screaming, "Daddy! Daddy!"

A door slammed and Ted shuddered. His eyes opened wide.

"You BASTARD COP! LET ME OUT!"

Ted looked across the cell block and saw a woman. Slowly, realizing her words were unheard by the Sheriff, she looked over to Ted. "Hey, Chief. Got any smokes?"

Ted was almost lifeless as he stared at her. After a moment, he rolled over, his back to the woman.

She hissed, "Men. You're all pricks."

He had heard that before, from someone who had once taken his breath away with her beauty and had captured his heart so completely that he could not have imagined life without her.

CHAPTER 2

YES, YOUR HONOR

He was probably wearing a bow tie under the black robe, Ted thought as he stood before the local magistrate. This man who would judge him seemed very efficient as he looked through a file. To Ted, a bow tie would symbolize neatness and order.

"What are you doing in Colorado, Mr. Rising Sun?"

The judge looked over the edge of the bench at Ted and seemed sincerely curious.

"Looking for work, your honor."

The judge turned his attention back to the file for a moment and read aloud. "Silver Star, Purple Heart, Presidential Unit Citation, Combat Infantryman's Badge, and on and on." He looked over the bench again. "You were a sergeant. With your background, finding work should be easy."

"Maybe for some," Ted replied.

"Mr. Rising Sun, you have a distinguished service record. In light of that, I am going to look upon you with leniency."

Genuinely, Ted responded. "Thank you, your honor."

The judge accepted Ted's sincerity but launched into a Civics lesson. "The Civil Rights Act that just became law may give Indians the right to buy liquor, but let me make something very clear to you. This community does not abide by drunkenness in public. Another display from you like this. . . . "

Ted was looking directly at the judge but the words had quickly become background noise. After years in the military and many life-threatening experiences in combat, the disciplinary words of some natty practitioner of the law were not going to hold Ted's attention. Not on this day.

The story of the Sand Creek massacre was still playing in his thoughts and, in this moment, it was very easy for Ted to allow his grandmother's words to envelop him. "Morning Star believed we had to learn the white man's way in order to survive the changing world. We gave ourselves over to their promise, but they would not let us live with grass and buffalo on the land of our ancestors."

Grandmother was born before the end of the Indian Wars and had been given the name "Holding Woman" as a child. When she told her stories to Ted, they were the unvarnished images of an adolescent who had witnessed what she spoke of. She had experienced every step of the relocation of her people from the north to the Indian Territories, in what is now Oklahoma, and had barely survived their desperate flight to their homeland, one year later.

The many years of fighting were to have ended with the signing of earlier treaties, the last of which had given the Northern Cheyenne an open plains reservation. But gold was discovered in the Black Hills and the railroads brought more Europeans west. The Cheyenne and the Sioux were unluckily in the way of expansion and progress. This led to an attempt by the government to buy back the reservation land from the Indians, who simply did not want to sell. After all, this had been their ancestors land. The idea of taking money for what had originally been given the Indian by the Great Mystery, God to the white man, was not to be comprehended. And, they had signed a treaty with the government that granted them the land—land that was already theirs.

The refusal to sell led to Custer's foolish and aggressive attempt to drive the Sioux and Cheyenne from the Little Bighorn. That decision ultimately cost the infamous general his life as well as those of his entire command. What followed was a buildup of military force under the command of General George Crook, the numbers of which simply overwhelmed the Sioux, Cheyenne, and all the plains Indians.

Crook, however, was respected by the Northern Cheyenne and considered to be a voice that could be trusted. In the autumn of 1877, the general gave his word, promising Morning Star that if the great Chief's people would agree to live in the southern "Indian Territory," all their needs would be provided for by the government. The general went further to promise that if this relocation did not suit their needs, the Cheyenne would be allowed to return north after one year. So it was with such confidence that Morning Star agreed to have his people walk from Nebraska to Oklahoma. His faith in General Crook was well placed. The general, as a representative of Washington, truly believed his promise to Morning Star would be kept.

In the Indian Territory, Morning Star's people were greeted by their Southern Cheyenne cousins. But it was immediately apparent that food was scarce. The unfamiliar land was parched by a long summer sun. The Northern Cheyenne were hunters and gatherers. Dry land does not attract grazing animals such as buffalo. Making matters worse, the reservation was overpopulated and the provisions supplied these people by the government were not increased to allow for new arrivals.

A year of starvation, disease, and death followed. The time came when Morning Star and his people could wait no longer, for death would surely take them all. And so it was this history that Grandmother had lived and thus formed her view of life.

Ted stood tall in front of the authority of the court but only heard the words of his grandmother. "We walked for a hundred sleeps, to the barren land. And when the moon of the drying grass came again, the promised year in the barren land was over. Morning Star and Little Wolf, the warrior Chief of the Crooked Lance, went to the agent in charge of the reservation."

The Crooked Lance Society was one of six Cheyenne military societies. The others were the Kit-Fox Men, the Red Shields, the Dog Soldiers, the Bow String Men, and the Crazy Dogs.

The images his grandmother gave of that day were so complete Ted could see tall young U.S. Cavalry Lieutenant Lawton, along with the post surgeon, and the agent in charge of the Indian Territory Agency, John Miles. They were seated and in some kind of argument when Morning Star and Little Wolf entered the office. The Chiefs were accompanied by Edmond Guerrier, one of the survivors of the Sand Creek massacre, now working as an interpreter for the military. It was September of 1878 at the Fort Reno headquarters.

Lawton was holding a report in front of Miles. His words were angry and biting. "My report to General Pope."

Miles thumbed through the papers as Lawton continued. "The Cheyenne women and children are sick for want of food!" He looked over to Morning Star and Little Wolf, both men gaunt from starvation. He turned back to Miles, "I demand to know why."

"We've had some shortages" offered Miles.

Lawton found the cavalier comment unthinkable. "Shortages?"

"Just . . . shortages . . . " Miles tone was an attempt to be more reassuring.

"What do you mean, Agent Miles?"

Miles put down the report and looked up at Lawton. Morning Star and Little Wolf observed this show of anger and frustration as Guerrier interpreted.

"Shortages. Beef, 700,000 pounds; coffee, 35,000 pounds; bacon, 30,000 pounds; flour, 340,000 pounds. Simple shortages." Miles figured his point was made.

The post surgeon added, "We get no medical supplies. No quinine. How can I treat malaria? Over seventy of their people have died in the short year since the army brought them here. And now a measles epidemic has struck. This is a pest camp. A graveyard! I am a doctor, and I cannot help them because you don't give me the tools I need."

Lawton stuttered, "But, our manifests record shipments of those missing supplies."

Miles quickly countered, "I know. But they never get to us. I continue to ask General Pope to push Washington for an increase in our allotment."

"And having the disappearing supplies found," added Lawton.

Morning Star stopped Guerrier from interpreting, then slowly stood. He was regal and wise, as one would expect a great leader to be.

"We came from our homeland in the north on the word of your General Crook. We know nothing of supplies. My people hunt the grasslands for the great buffalo. We are strangers to this dry country. We wish to be on land where we can make our home, and send our children to school to learn about your way of life. We want permission to go north, as General Crook promised when we agreed to try this land."

Little Wolf was impatient with dialog. He simply wanted action and so he interrupted. "We must return to our home in the north."

Miles shrugged, "I cannot give you that permission."

Little Wolf did not hesitate, "General Crook gave us permission!"

"Stay another year and I'll see what can be done for you. But please, make no trouble." Miles had pleaded like this before. It meant nothing now, especially to Little Wolf.

"NO! Before another year has passed, we may all be dead."

Morning Star spoke again, with a calm to his voice that fit his stately appearance. "Till the dry earth, you say. But the plows you promise never come. And while my people die, you ask they wait another year? My people carry the burial rocks now, everyday. If we die here, no one will speak our name. If we die going north to our land, the Cheyenne *will be* remembered. Now the moon of the drying grass has come. No, we are going. We will not sneak away. We want you to know, we are going home."

Miles was becoming uncomfortable with this. "You cannot do this. Do you understand the army will pursue you, and bring you back here?" He turned to Guerrier. "Do they understand?" He turned back to Morning Star and again implored, "Do you understand?"

Suddenly Ted heard the judge sternly repeat the words, "Do you understand me, Mr. Rising Sun?"

Ted was lost in the moment of seven decades earlier. His expression did not change as he answered the question. "Yes."

After a long look at Ted, the judge pounded the gavel.

CHAPTER 3
THE LAND OF PROMISE

Gentle hills covered with stands of pine surrounded Lame Deer, Montana. The paved highway was crossed by the one dirt street that housed the town. The general store and post office were housed in the same solitary structure. There was a sign, too, complete with a few bullet holes. It read, *WEL-COME TO LAME DEER, MONTANA, and THE NORTHERN CHEYENNE INDIAN RESERVATION.*

In a clearing behind the general store, a chain-linked construction yard took up about an acre. The foreman was closing and locking the gate, which disappointed several of the men gathered outside the fence, including Ted, and his friend Sylvester. Some of the men were hanging on the fence with fingers through the links, almost as if in prison looking out.

Sylvester asked the foreman, "What about our jobs?"

"Yeah, what are we supposed to do?" grumbled others.

The foreman seemed to know this drill well, offering just enough sympathy. "Sorry, boys. You know, Eisenhower canceled all reservation contracts. There's just no more building. The days of the Civil Conservation Corps are long over. I just got the word from Denver. The company is pulling out. Real sorry."

Hearing that, Ted knew there was nothing to discuss. This guy was just doing his job. Ted turned and walked away. Sylvester ran after him.

"What are you going to do?"

Ted didn't break his stride. "Maybe I'll find work in Denver. I don't know. I gotta do something."

"What about your family?"

Ted quickly responded, "I'll take them with me."

The sun was setting in a crimson sky. A very hungry dog ravaged through a trash pile along the dirt roadway that passed several rough wood shacks. In the backyard of each was an outhouse. There were *no* power poles on this residential block. In fact, there was no power in all of Lame Deer. And yet, it was 1954.

In the shack, Ted was seated at a makeshift table across from his wife, Helen. An nearly empty bottle of wine and glass sat in front of her. To one side were Ted's two daughters, six-year-old Ruthie and four-year-old Myra. They were both unbathed and eating from an open can of beans.

Home for this family was one room with an unfinished interior. A rough wood floor, exposed wall studs, newspaper used to cover the seams in the exterior siding, and well-worn furniture completed the room. A couple of oil lamps gave light to the otherwise dark interior. There was no running water, no bath.

Ted was uncomfortable as he was trying to explain the job circumstances he had experienced. "Helen, I don't know what else to do."

Helen's reply was quick, "Well, you ain't takin' these girls."

"I said, we can all go."

"And live on what? What are you going to do in Denver?"

She poured the rest of the wine in her glass and took a drink.

Ted offered a little hope "There's construction down there. I'll find work. There's got to be more opportunity there. . . . "

She cut him off, "In white man's world?"

"Hey, I did good in the Army. Or have you forgotten?"

This time she cut his legs off. "A lotta good your medals do now."

He just stared at her, anger building.

And then to test him, she threw it out again. "Like I said, I ain't going to Denver."

Ted got up, grabbed his jacket, and bolted out the door.

Helen yelled out, "Yeah, just leave. You BASTARD!"

Ted was a few steps from the door heading for the street as Helen, with the girls crying by her side, stepped out.

"Daddy! Daddy!" the girls called.

Helen screamed at him, "I'll never let you have these girls. Never. NEVER!"

He turned back to her, "You don't know what you're saying.

You're drunk."

The girls were becoming hysterical as they continued to call, "Daddy, Daddy."

Helen stepped back in the house, pulling the girls with her, slamming the door closed.

As he walked on, those words kept playing in his thoughts, "Daddy! Daddy!"

CHAPTER 4
MILE HIGH CITY

A light snow was falling. The pavement was not quite frozen, at least not yet. Those pretty soft flakes melted as they hit the blacktop in the alley. Had it been a little later in the year they would have made a soft blanket of white to cover the grime and hide some of the sins of big city life. That day, however, melting snow and the filth of the alley combined to become gray slush.

The early morning trash truck was making its first downtown run of the day. Over the years, city residents have gotten used to the familiar sound of hydraulic arms driven by pistons, diesel engines, clanging trash cans emptying against cold steel bins and, of course, the smell of man's litter. The stuff comes in all forms, especially when left by city dwellers. Yet, one man's garbage is sometimes another's treasure.

As the truck moved toward Fifth Street, it left a wake of noise and odors. But for the street people, it left a hoard of discarded newspaper and cardboard that they turned into bedding. From under such a pile of yesterday's all important headlines, Ted stirred. The start of another day had arrived with as little promise as the day before and probably the day after. But he got up and did his best to prepare for the world.

The toll from living on the streets of Denver was showing on Ted's face. He was developing what an artist might refer to as real character. Lines that ran from the eyes, mouth, across the forehead, and down the cheeks were a sort of road map, telling something about where Ted Rising Sun had been.

Ted noticed a half-smoked cigarette lying under the protection of a ledge. He picked it up, put it to his mouth without concern, and pulled out his Zippo. He cupped his unsteady hand around the lighter and managed to get the cigarette lit. His hands were once very strong. Now they were cracked from the cold air and wet nights found on the streets. After a deep drag, he moved down the alley. He was heading towards the promise of warmth from the sunlight that bathed the west side of the block.

Ted waited for a passing car then crossed the street. The snow clouds had blown on, leaving the clear blue sky and a strong reflective glare off the wet pavement. Blue skies usually mean cold air in this country. Ted found his way out of the shadows and into the warm light.

A middle-aged man wearing an overcoat and carrying a paper cup of coffee passed Ted on his left without giving him a look. It was not that Ted was invisible. It was simply that eye contact meant acknowledgment. But the man shifted the coffee cup to his right hand just before he passed Ted. Why, Ted wondered, as he watched the quick steps moving on towards the corner. Ted knew the man had seen him. Out of the corner of his eyes the man had prepared himself to fend off another homeless person who he was sure would ask him for money. Just before the man reached the corner he took a quick glimpse over his shoulder to make sure he wasn't being followed, and then disappeared. Ted unconsciously straightened his hair as he moved down the block.

The foundation for a commercial building was being poured on an excavated commercial lot down the street. At the edge of the lot, a contractor's office trailer was parked. As heavy trucks and equipment moved in and out of the lot, the construction boss was reviewing site plans with his foreman.

Ted approached the busy men, putting on as friendly a face as he could muster. "Excuse me," he muttered. Immediately he realized they would never hear him unless he spoke up. "Excuse me!"

The boss glimpsed Ted, then flat ignored him. He turned his attention to the foreman. "Jack, bring it out another twelve feet, to right here."

The boss leaned over with a aerosol paint can and sprayed an X in white. He set the can next to the mark.

"Got it, boss." With that quick acknowledgment, the foreman walked off.

Ted once again tried to get the boss' attention. "Excuse me, sir?"

The boss turned to Ted and took in his rough condition.

The busy man was not thrilled with the intruder in his workplace. In what seemed like an eternity, Ted waited for the man to respond. He could see that the boss looked at him from head to toe.

Finally a response. "Yeah, what is it?"

"I was wondering if you need men?"

The boss looked a little incredulous. "We pick our men from the union hall. You a member of the local?" He threw that at Ted with a raised eyebrow.

"No."

"Can't help you, then, Cochise."

As the boss started to turn away, Ted tried another approach. "What about odd work? Anything?"

The boss turned back, looked around for a second and then answered with a question. "You got any tools? Have any construction experience?"

"I don't have tools with me, but. . . . "

At that point, the man was done. "There's a shelter down the block. Maybe they can help you." He was looking at Ted in a way that made him feel small. "What the hell ya doing off the reservation? You oughta get work where you belong." Before Ted might answer, the boss walked off.

Knowing there was nothing for him there, Ted answered softly, almost as if ashamed. "There is no work . . . on the reservation."

But the boss could not have heard him with all the equipment moving. And even if he had, he would have ignored the "Red Man" anyway.

Ted stood motionless for a moment. Then he leaned over, picked up the aerosol paint can and hid it up his sleeve. He looked around but, of course, no one was paying any attention to him. After a moment, Ted walked away.

His bed of cardboard was still in the alley, but the newspapers had scattered with the breeze. Ted was more concerned with the contents of a trash can. He was digging for something. After a few moments, he removed a small brown, very dirty paper bag.

Ted stepped away, moving further into the shadows of the alley. In a protected corner, he dropped down and leaned back against the building. His look was forlorn. What was the purpose in life anyway? It all seemed pointless.

A moment passed before he placed the bag to his mouth and blew into it, expanding the brown paper. Then he pulled the aerosol paint can from his jacket and stuck its nozzle into the bag, spraying paint in it for a few seconds. With no thought, Ted put the bag to his face and deeply inhaled.

After a few moments, his eyes rolled and his head fell back against the wall. His hand, still holding the bag, dropped from his mouth. His exposed face revealed traces of white paint on his nostrils and his lips. His eyes were glazing over.

A light drizzle began. Rainwater spit on Ted's face and seemed to bring him back to consciousness. He leaned forward with a jolt, mumbling, "Quiet! He's out there, in the trees."

Ted squinted, looking out from the alley towards a tree that overhung a fence. Water collected in his hair from the drizzle and ran down his forehead. Ted looked on at the pavement in front of him. "We can't run. He'll see us."

Ted's eyes closed for a moment and his head dropped. Then, just as suddenly, he opened his eyes and reached for the paint can. He put the nozzle into the bag, sprayed for a moment, then covered his mouth again, inhaling deeply.

After a few seconds the bag dropped, revealing more paint on his face. Ted slowly tilted over until he was laying on his side. But deep inside he was awake again in another time and place.

Rain was falling lightly, wind gusts were spitting the water in Ted's very alert face. It was North Korea. Ted was in camouflage and battle helmet, taking cover from enemy fire. He was a sergeant in command of a small outfit that was pinned down by a sniper. Two of his men had been killed. Six other soldiers were crouched in the mud, trying to keep protected from the sniper firing from somewhere ahead. Brush and rock was all that protected these soldiers from the danger in a line of trees that were some seventy-five yards away. A clearing of twenty feet stood between their position and safety. The bodies of the two dead American soldiers were laying in that clearing, victims of the unseen enemy.

Ted was staring with intensity, watching the tree line. He barely breathed and remained absolutely still. He had tremendous power of concentration, learned well from his dad. His eyes were clear, his hands steady, his senses keen. He seemed to understand this kind of human conflict. His men were impatient, feeling the stress of being pinned down. They wanted to get a look. For Ted, it was a game between the hunted and the hunter. Corporal Kowalski, a fresh-faced young man, fired a couple of rounds without having a clue where to shoot. There was no return fire.

One of the younger soldiers turned to Ted. "Sarge, we can't just sit here."

Kowalski nervously interrupted. "I musta hit him."

Ted did not break his scan but simply gestured for the soldier to be quiet. His confidence went unappreciated in this moment.

Kowalski, nearest the clearing, looked out at the tree line then back to the others. He couldn't stand the pressure of the wait. He broke and ran. Even this did not distract Ted. Once Kowalski began to run, there was nothing Ted could do to protect him. Ten steps later a rifle shot exploded from the tree line, hitting Kowalski, dropping him.

Ted's eyes picked up something in the tree line. It was the slightest puff of blue smoke. Slowly, with great concentration, he took aim with his M-1 rifle. Every sensory element within his control was focused on this target, hidden behind layers of green. Those many times Ted had hunted with his dad, when he had learned to be one with his environment, had not been forgotten.

Ted squeezed off the round. It reported with the unmistakable smack of a body taking an impact. A moment of delay, and then they heard the body of the enemy falling from the trees.

Ted turned to his men. "NOW!"

The men were up and moving, making their way across the deadly twenty-foot span in an instant. Ted dropped to Kowalski's side to assist his young comrade. "You still with us?"

Kowalski struggled to get up. "Got me in the leg, High Hawk. Can't get up."

"We'll get you outta here."

Ted started to pick up Kowalski.

"That was a great shot. No wonderCuster never had a chance."

Ted grinned. "Be quiet or I'll leave you here."

Ted picked up Kowalski and carried him out of the clearing. The rain was still spitting in his face as a ray of sunlight cut through the overcast sky. The light got brighter until it was almost too much to look at.

A room slowly came into focus. Ted came out of what seemed like a long sleep. He was laying on a cot in a shelter, a white light hanging overhead. He focused on the light and then realized he had been dreaming about the war. He glanced across the room and saw that he was one of several such homeless men. Who knew what their lives had been, but their faces spoke of many trials.

Ted tried to get up but began coughing. It was very deep, rattling from way inside. This was the kind of cough that hurts. Gripping the sides of the cot, he was barely able to stop the involuntary choking that followed. The only way he managed was to take very short breaths until he felt his body relaxing.

Overcoming the cough all but knocked Ted out. He was breaking out in a sweat from the ordeal. As he began to feel in control of his breathing, he laid back. The light bothered him and he closed his eyes. As he did, an overexposed image of his two daughters that was almost completely white, came to his mind. They were playing and gleeful. Ted was pushing them on a long rope swing.

Sometime later Ted sat at a long table eating bread and drinking soup. His eyes were hollow but the clean, dry clothes he now wore made him feel better. He was keeping to himself. A priest approached him and sat across the table. He placed a manila envelope on the table.

"Ted. I'm Father Ryan."

"Father."

"How ya feeling?"

Ted thought about it for a moment. "Shaky."

"I'm surprised you're even up."

Ted managed a smile. "Figured I better eat while I could."

Father Ryan slid the envelope to Ted. "These things were in your pockets."

Ted peeked in the envelope and pulled out his Zippo lighter. It felt good in his hand.

"When did you get out of the service?" the priest asked.

"I was discharged a couple months ago. You know, when the war ended."

Father Ryan took a moment and then carefully replied. "When you finish eating, come to my office, will you?"

Ted did not challenge. "Okay, Father."

The priest moved on, stopping to visit with the other men. Ted watched for a moment. The priest was very friendly and he seemed very sincere as he spoke with each man. Eyes that were disillusioned with life welcomed the dialog with a man of the cloth. Ted thought, "Maybe there is a purpose to all this, all that we call life." Then he returned to his meal.

Father Ryan's office was very basic. A lone crucifix hung on the wall behind him. Ted had taken a seat across the desk and could not help but notice a wonderful photo of Knute Rockne and the 1928 Notre Dame football team hanging by itself.

"Did you ever meet him?" Ted asked.

The priest looked over to the picture with a warm memory.

"I was a freshman in thirty-one, his last season. Talk about inspiration."

He looked back at Ted and continued. "No coach will ever match his .881 winning average. It's a record that will stand for all time."

Ted thought about it for a moment. "I haven't seen a football game since I got out of the service. My outfit had some pretty good players."

"Ted, do you realize the war was over four years ago? It's 1958."

"No. That can't be. I've been looking for work. I've had some bad luck, but. . . . "

"When you came in here, you were totally incoherent. If you've been living like this, well, it's no wonder you don't know what day it is."

"But it's only been a couple of months since I. . . . " Ted spaced on the reality of those words. How could four years have gone by? Where did they go?

"I spoke to your father in Busby. You had his phone number in your wallet. He wants you to come home . . . to the reservation. Your children need you."

Ted's face revealed nothing. The priest said "Ted, your children. . . . "

"Daddy! Daddy!" Ted heard those words again; and as always, from deep within his body, he felt pain.

CHAPTER 5
GOING HOME

The road extended endlessly into the sinking sun. It always looked bigger to Ted in its final hours of the day. He never understood why. He felt the same about the rising moon. It would look huge on the horizon as it found its way past the wind-swept sand buttes but would diminish as it rose higher.

The Greyhound bus had been rolling west now for seven hours. Ted had been looking on at the endless miles of high plains, and counting those hours, those minutes. He had not seen Ruthie and Myra since that horrible day when he walked away from their cries at the porch. It had been their mother's screams from which he had fled. Would they ever understand? They would be ten and eight now. Four years gone, almost half their little lives. Would they even remember him? What would Helen have said to them about their father?

Helen, Helen. When she was younger, before the binges and the pain, she was beautiful. As much as Ted hated what life with her had become, he could not resist these thoughts of this woman. Her jet black hair, dark eyes, she was one of the last of the Northern Cheyenne beauties, the ones that caused the soldiers 100 years earlier to refer to the Cheyenne as "the beautiful people." There was a regal dignity in her profile that contrasted with a wildness in her eyes that spoke of her power. In days long since lost to her people, Helen would have been the prize of all women. For Private Ted Rising Sun, Helen was exactly that.

Ted was on leave, just out of boot camp when he first saw Helen. When they met, the attraction was so immediate and the passion so intense they could not be separated. Within those thirty days, before he reported for his WWII duty in the Army, they married. The young lovers did not realize that Helen was pregnant as Ted stepped on the troop train. A year-and-a-half later, he came home to his first daughter, Ruthie, right after McArthur accepted the Japanese surrender.

Ted wondered what it must have been like for the Emperor of Japan to surrender his empire and country. But then, what must it have been like for Ted's great grandfather to surrender his country, way of life, and people? History books discuss Japan's capitulation, but at the time little was written to consider the American Indian's submission.

Ted looked around the bus. Half the seats were empty.

He pulled out his smokes and lit up. He kept opening his Zippo and lighting it. Somehow it was reassuring to hear the sound of the top as it opened, and then see the flame. But the best part was the sound of the top as it closed. There was an authority to it.

He rested his head and took another drag. Grandmother's words took over his thoughts once again. "Someday they will ask, and they will listen, and you will tell our story."

He looked out at the long shadows that interrupted the warm orange light casting itself upon the landscape in these final minutes of that day.

Grandmother's words continued. "Morning Star knew that to save the children was everything."

Her words dissolved into images once again as Ted returned to his journey with his ancestors. Morning Star and Little Wolf were silently leading their 350 people north. The stark landscape was bathed in red from the rising sun that day. Without a glance, they left behind their standing lodges and almost everything they had carried there by foot one year earlier. Slipping away undetected through long morning shadows, it was the ninth day of September, 1878. It was the day the Northern Cheyenne would start their incredible journey home.

Ted lost himself in those thoughts, Grandmother's words, as if she were sitting beside him telling the story for the first time. "I was five years old the day Morning Star told us we were returning to our home. Our hearts looked and longed for the country where we were born."

Under the watchful eyes of the military detachment assigned to Fort Reno, the Cheyenne disappeared into the northern horizon unnoticed.

"We were only three-hundred-fifty. All we wanted was a little ground where we could live. Morning Star knew that his people would be wiped off the earth if he did not lead us north. It was his duty to save the tribe."

It took a full day for the fort commander to get over the fact that the Cheyenne had just disappeared. He sent word to his commander that they were preparing an immediate pursuit. In truth, it was not until four days had passed that the military caught sight of the Cheyenne.

Morning Star and his people had crossed to the north of a dry riverbed. Four canyons crisscrossed at this point. Having made their way to the top of the cliff, through a narrow draw Morning Star and Little Wolf looked to the southern horizon and saw the approaching dust cloud of the cavalry. They quickly positioned warriors in defense, hiding them within cedar brakes. Those with bows and arrows were placed closer and those with a rifle further back. The old men, women, and children were moved beyond range of this position, taking the few horses they had with them.

Grandmother continued in Ted's thoughts. "We were driven by a common will. We could show no mercy to our nerves, our muscles, or our few horses." He knew in a time such as this, there could be only one purpose: Survival of the tribe.

Morning Star and Little Wolf counseled with their young braves led by Little Finger Nail. They called him "The Nail." Morning Star's sons, Bull Hump and Little Hump, also joined in with Little Wolf's sons, Pawnee and Wooden Thigh.

The Nail spoke with respect. "Tell us, old ones, what can we do? The Blue Coats are many."

Since Little Wolf was still of fighting age, the younger warriors had much respect for his experience and waited for his answer.

"These Blue Coats will be blinded by the breaking of the white father's promise. Long Hair Custer was blinded when he broke the promise of peace he gave to the Chiefs in the Sacred Arrow Lodge. That is why he died."

Morning Star added, "It was the power of the Sacred Arrows and Sacred Hat at the Little Bighorn that made Custer foolish."

Ted, as would all Cheyenne, understood the power of the Sacred Arrows. A ceremony was performed each year over a four day period at the time of summer solstice. A sacred bundle was a part of that ceremony of renewal that empowered the men. The bundle was a hat, made from the skin and hair of a buffalo cow, and four arrows, two for hunting and two for battle. Morning Star knew that it was the power from this sacred bundle that defeated Custer. The young general had violated the treaty that gave the land to the Indians. But worse, he dishonored his own word given to the Chiefs. Ironic that it was the search for gold within the Black Hills and Little Bighorn which led Custer, a man known to the Cheyenne as "Yellow Hair," to his famous death.

Little Hump was looking at the closeness of the approaching dust cloud. "But the Blue Coats are joined by Arapahos and Blue Clouds."

Morning Star calmly responded, "Yes, they are in this, too. Our old allies. We have fought off people from our own families before."

The Nail acknowledged, "They have Cheyenne with them."

But here Morning Star's face changed as he issued a stern warning. "We will say nothing of this to the women and children. It will do them no good to realize we fight some of our own."

Bull Hump added, "Man has to die sometime."

The simplicity of the comment was not lost on the old ones. Surely the hand of fate was being tempted in the act of this flight from the pursuing cavalry.

Little Wolf knew it was time to take position. "Now go. Don't shoot foolishly. We have little ammunition."

Morning Star added, "We will need it later to defend the helpless ones."

The Nail was proud to be a part of this council. "*Hou!*"

And with that, the braves scattered, disappearing from view. Morning Star looked up at the sun. "Good medicine."

Little Wolf looked as well. "*Maheo* will blind them."

Morning Star spotted a blanket signal from across the river. "Look."

The rising smoke clouds were clear against the sky.

Morning Star was at once hopeful. "We will speak to them. The scout will help the Blue Coats understand us."

Little Wolf was not as optimistic. He followed Morning Star as he started down the bluff towards the riverbed. From the other side, two Army scouts—a Blue Cloud and Edmond Guerrier—were moving to join the Chiefs. At the bottom, Guerrier and the Indian crossed to Morning Star and Little Wolf.

Guerrier spoke first. "My friends, please listen. The white leader is anxious. He wants to turn you back. If you continue, there will be much trouble."

Little Wolf was impatient. "We are away from our Southern Cheyenne brothers' land now. If blood must spill, it will stain this earth, not theirs."

Guerrier answered. "Our southern brothers thank you. But I have seen what the Blue Coats will do. I survived Sand Creek."

Morning Star's reaction was immediate. "If my people are to die, it will not be malaria or other white man's sicknesses that kill us. It will be because we hold General Crook to his promise that we may return to our land."

"But Miles did not give permission for you to leave."

Morning Star repeated the terms. "General Crook promised at Fort Robinson that if the south was not good, we could return north."

Little Wolf firmly warned Guerrier. "We want to go in peace. But let the soldiers know that if they fight us, we will fight them . . . and anyone who joins with them."

Guerrier gestured to the ridge behind him. "They are many."

"And we are Cheyenne." Morning Star added that with a resolute tone that told Guerrier the conversation was over.

After a long moment, Guerrier and the Blue Cloud withdrew. Perhaps the next time they looked at each other, it would be in battle. Morning Star and Little Wolf started up the northern edge.

Some 200 yards north, on the flats behind the braves, Morning Star's wives, Pawnee Woman and Short One (it was common then for a Cheyenne Chief to have more than one wife), and his two daughters, thirteen-year-old Broken Foot Woman and five-year-old Holding Woman; along with Little Wolf's wife, Feather on the Head, and their daughter, Pretty

Walker; and The Nail's wife, Singing Cloud, waited with apprehension for the sound of the battle. They were with the old ones that Morning Star had referred to as "the helpless ones."

Pretty Walker was showing her apprehension. "I don't understand why the Blue Coats are following us. All we want to do is go home."

Pawnee Woman was the strongest voice of the women and greatly loved. "Do not be afraid, my sisters. There are many among us who have stood up to the soldiers. Our men are brave. You are Cheyenne."

At that point, Short One began a chant in Cheyenne.

Proudly we follow the path of Morning Star. Many snows he has spoken for peace. Carrying the pipe of peace in his hand, like others the bow and the shooting guns.

At that moment, the cavalry bugle sounded the charge, bringing an abrupt end to the song and with it, the knowledge that some were about to die.

Morning Star and Little Wolf were still moving up the cliff face as the charge began. There were several soldiers on foot and a few on horseback, leading the charge. Captain Joseph Rendlebrock, his blond face burned from sun and whiskey, was out front. The soldiers broke into the clear, guns blaring. The sun was in their eyes as they aimed at the fleeing Chiefs.

The Nail and Bull Hump saw their two Chiefs' immediate danger. They sighted their rifles on the puffs of blue smoke rising from the soldiers' positions and returned fire into the brush.

Morning Star and Little Wolf hurried up the cliff, bullets striking around them, red dust rising in the sunlight. As the soldiers charged, the two Chiefs were nearing the cliff top.

The soldiers were within range of arrows and clean shots. The Cheyenne let arrows fly and opened rifle fire, hitting several soldiers, both on horseback and those on foot. Chaos was setting in among their ranks. The sun was making it impossible for them to see up the cliff, and they were totally exposed to the line of fire from those they pursued.

Morning Star and Little Wolf safely rejoined The Nail. Morning Star spoke first. "You did well. The Blue Coats are confused."

Little Wolf added again, "Don't shoot foolishly. You have little to give your rifles."

The warriors continued to fend off the soldiers. It was an afternoon of mayhem for the cavalry. Indeed, *Maheo* had interceded. The sun stayed in the soldiers' eyes, making it impossible to fight with any effectiveness. They were unable to advance on the Cheyenne position, despite their relentless effort. As the battle raged, the soldiers lost several men.

Grandmother's voice spoke to Ted with pride. "Our people were defended by sixty braves. We held back hundreds of soldiers and lost not one. During the night, we slipped away to the north."

The steady rhythm of bus tires crossing the seams of the pavement covering a bridge brought Ted out of his thoughts. He gazed out the window, the passing lights reflecting off his dark eyes. Seated next to Ted was a nineteen-year-old soldier, dressed in his very new Army uniform. Ted was unaware of the younger man. He had been asleep at the last stop when the young man boarded. As Ted lit a cigarette with his trusted Zippo, the soldier noticed the emblem on the lighter.

"Say, can I get a light?"

Ted offered the lighter without looking. The soldier took it and lit up. As he handed it back to Ted, he tried to open up the conversation. "Thanks. Which outfit were you in?"

Without looking Ted replied, "Twenty-fourth Infantry."

The soldier got excited. "Hundred and first Airborne. On my first leave."

"Enjoy it."

The young man did not let it rest. "When'd you get out?"

Ted took a deep breath. He really did *not* want the distraction. "A while back."

"See any action?"

"A little." With that Ted turned his head towards the window. His eyes took in the blanket of stars above as he drifted into his thoughts, leaving the young soldier to continue.

"Those Commies. They got that Sputnik satellite up there spying on us. And the H-bomb. I mean Kruschchev said the Ruskies would bury us. Ain't gonna happen on my watch." He went on for awhile but soon Ted did not hear a word. He was taken up with a journey in progress. Morning Star's quest for the freedom and dignity of the Cheyenne was taking a different form in Ted's thoughts. For all the years he had heard this story, it was only now that he began to feel an intertwined connection of spirits. Somehow there was to be a purpose in Ted's life. It was certainly to be more than his military honors, more than his domestic plight, or raising his children. No, it had something to do with being back with his people.

Unless you live in the country, away from the influence of big city skylines, the darkness of a moonless night cannot be fathomed. This was one of those nights, but not rare in the nineteenth century. In the days before Thomas Edison found the magic of electricity and the west became populated with big cities like the ones to the east, nights when the sky was as black as coal and mottled with shimmering diamonds were as common as the clear water in the streams or the unaltered horizon and clean air.

On this particular night, no shadows were cast from the moon for it was in a shadow itself. So it would take a people who were one with the earth to find their way in the darkness without fear.

Morning Star and his people moved to the edge of the tall grass near the Platte River. Little Hump, The Nail, and other young warriors walked beside their ponies, the palm of one hand gently calming their equine partner's natural apprehension. The children, exhausted and hungry, whimpered from the pain of the never-ending travel. Mothers and grandmothers encouraged the little ones on. Morning Star and Little Wolf looked towards distant voices of soldiers. Morning Star turned to Pawnee Woman and Short One with a look they immediately understood. His eyes clearly said the children must be quiet. Were it not for the fact that the soldiers across the river were so relaxed and noisy in their evening jaw around the fire, one of them might have heard the Cheyenne children.

Little Wolf signaled Pawnee, Wooden Thigh, and other braves to stay with the helpless ones. Then he and Morning Star moved forward silently, disappearing into the tall grass.

At the river's edge, Morning Star and Little Wolf could see a series of twenty large campfires on the other side. Soldiers were milling about each fire, relaxing after the evening meal. It was still and the night air carried their voices, so it seemed these military men were very close. A troop train stood in rest, its steam engine boiler still stoked, belching, and groaning. The firelight revealed the cold steel of a howitzer mounted in the center of a flatcar hitched to the waiting train.

Morning Star took note of the position of each camp. The distance between the fires was the same except the two in the middle. There was a dark space in the center of that long line of campfires wide enough that it caught his attention. He whispered to Little Wolf, "There, in the center. We could pass. The Blue Coats would never expect us."

"Blue! Blue, goddamn dog wandered off again." The words rolled across the river from one of the soldiers and at first seemed to be directed at the two Chiefs. At that same instant, Morning Star and Little Wolf heard the almost silent sniffing of a dog very close to them. Little Wolf reacted and with no hesitation sprung towards it. In the darkness he landed on a dog, grabbing it by the muzzle. The struggle lasted only a moment as Little Wolf snapped the dog's neck.

Unknowingly, the soldier called out again. "Blue! Blue, where the hell are you?"

Little Wolf silently and respectfully laid the now limp dog to rest in the grass, gently stoking the side of its face as if putting it down for a sleep. He thought, "What master would leave such a fine animal to the dangers of the night?"

The soldier, Corporal Smith, was continuing his search for Blue. Just beyond him a group huddled around the fire was watching. A voice from the campfire called to the soldier. "Smith, that dog of yours is chasing some coyote bitch. I told ya to tie him up."

From the darkness, a tall young officer approached the soldier. "Smith, either go out into that darkness you let your dog wander into, and find him, or stay here. But whatever you do, shut up. Your dog is not the only one who might hear you."

Smith, now standing at attention replied. "Yes, sir."

The officer turned and walked back towards his tent as the discouraged soldier returned to the campfire.

The fires were now mostly embers. A lone sentry stood his post near the outfit's many tethered horses. He had long given up looking for anything. What was there to see in all that blackness? The cigarettes he rolled and smoked would get him through the night while the others slept. Another sentry stood on the flatcar bed next to the howitzer. He was fascinated with the sky. A mere seventy yards away an entire nation they were hunting, was silently slipping past them.

Morning Star watched as silhouettes crossed silently from the grass cover on the south to the river's edge and then on to the other side, disappearing over the sandy ridge.

A slight noise from the grass was immediately followed by the call of a lonely coyote. Neither of the sentries could have imagined the boldness of this move, but then neither of these men was Cheyenne.

One by one the Cheyenne passed Morning Star. Men led their horses, silently communicating confidence to their four-legged brothers. Children were carried by mothers and grandmothers. Their focus was singular: Cross the river and then the railroad tracks. They would not allow themselves to be distracted by the campfires and the danger of those encampments they were in the heart of.

Grandmother's words had filled the image with great detail. "In the moon of the falling leaves, the river was quiet. The horses understood and made no sound as we crossed the gravel bed of the railroad. A Cheyenne is part of his pony, able to communicate his desire with just a touch of his hand, a slight caress, a whispered word."

The last of the long line of Cheyenne passed Morning Star and then he too disappeared to the north. As his pony passed from the river soil to the sandy bank, a gust of wind came up and dusted his foot tracks. *Maheo* was taking each step with Morning Star.

The morning brought chaos to the soldier encampment. Smith had found Blue and with him the evidence that the Cheyenne had evaded the net cast by the Army. A sharp windstorm that was blowing sand into the men and their horses made it nearly impossible for them to move. Officers barked commands as soldiers fought the elements while they broke down the camp. As they loaded up, the horses fought their mounts, not wanting any part of the sand that blew in their eyes. The men coughed and spit; shielding their mouths was almost pointless.

Grandmother went on. "Sweet Medicine brought the winds."

Morning Star led his weary people headfirst into the blowing sand. Pawnee Woman followed him with their daughters in tow. Short One carried the family's few precious items in leather bags hoisted on her back. Their movement was of steady determination. For them there would be no thought of turning away from the stinging sand.

And Grandmother added, "Sweet Medicine kept us moving."

Somewhere behind them a column of cavalry tried to move through knee-deep sand. But just ahead of the soldiers the sand filled in and disguised the northbound tracks of the fleeing Cheyenne. The Great Mystery would make sure there was no trail left to follow.

On the horizon, the sun's red glow filtered through the sand-filled air. This was a day orchestrated by something greater than man, and none of these soldiers would forget it.

Grandmother punctuated the story with a final and succinct thought. "And Sweet Medicine discouraged the soldiers."

This, most clearly, had been accomplished, for the cavalry column turned and headed south, the wind now at their backs. As the officer in command took the long ride toward the Platte, he kept replaying the events of the preceding twenty-four hours. How would he explain to his commander, General Crook, that 300 Cheyenne had walked through his camp undetected? How would he explain that his cavalry of hundreds and his steam-driven locomotive with its flatcar-mounted howitzer had been rendered impotent by a band of starving, unequipped, and outnumbered "savages"?

In the few hours of one dark night, this unit of the U.S. Army was given a lesson in military tactics never to be forgotten. The experience was beyond the grasp of the military hunters. The fleeing Indians, pursued by numbers into the thousands, had no desire to harm the Blue Coats. They simply wanted to go home.

CHAPTER 6
REUNION

It was sunset as Ted stepped off the bus. The aspen had already dropped their leaves in expectation of the coming snows. As the Greyhound rolled on, the bleakness of his hometown greeted him. To anyone else it might have seemed a depressed outpost, but to Ted it was home. He was in the heart of Lame Deer, the intersection of the main highway and the crossing dirt road that was Main Street.

Night had set in by the time Ted stepped on the front porch of his father's home. The door opened and Oliver looked on Ted with a warm smile.

"Hello, son."

"Dad."

The two men took each other in, each happy the moment had arrived.

"Well, come in."

Ted entered the very modest two-bedroom home. A fire was burning in the potbelly stove and gave off a comforting kind of heat. Beyond the front room, the house opened to the kitchen and dining area. A tabletop AM radio quietly played swing music, and a half read weekly newspaper lay on the floor alongside Oliver's easy chair.

"Where are your things?" asked Oliver.

"This is it."

"You've lost weight."

Ted completed that thought. "And a lot of time."

"It's good to have you home."

Oliver shook Ted's hand strongly. As he did, Ted saw Myra, now eight years old, looking at him from around the corner of the kitchen.

Four years suddenly struck him. "Is that Myra?"

She was very coy, her big dark eyes looking on at her father.

"Isn't she pretty?" Oliver encouraged her, "Come here, Myra. Say hello."

She was not sure what to do or how to act so she stood still. Elizabeth, Ted's mother, called out from the kitchen, just out of view from the men.

"Oliver, who are you talking to?"

"Why don't you come out and see for yourself?"

Elizabeth wasted no time and rushed into view, a dish-towel still in her hand. "Oh, dear."

It looked as if she was going to burst into tears as she ran to Ted. Hugging him, she admitted, "Ted, we have missed you."

The emotion of all this was awkward for Ted. Though pleased to see his mother and father, he was still looking at Myra. After a long moment, Elizabeth let go of him.

He turned to his mother. "I've missed you, too, Mom."

Myra was still staring as Elizabeth moved to her. She took the little girl's hand and led her to a meeting place with her dad. "Myra, your daddy's home."

Ted hunkered down to his little girl's eye level. After a moment of looking at each other, he reached out to her.

"Do you remember me, Myra?"

Myra nodded.

"You sure have gotten big—and, I sure have missed you and Ruthie."

Myra blurted out. "Me too."

Ted pulled her in for a big hug which lasted almost a minute. Her warmth was soothing and reassuring. Then he stood up, still holding her. They rocked back and forth a little and her smile got bigger and bigger. It felt right to Ted, and he wondered how he had survived without that feeling. Then he put her down.

"And where's your sister?" he asked her.

"With Grandmother."

Elizabeth added. "They're in the next room for Ruthie's nightly lessons with Grandma."

Ted looked down at Myra. "Will you take me to them, please?"

"Yes," she blurted with the wonderful kind of authority possessed by a child who knows the safety of her home.

Myra waited, though. She wanted this to happen a special way. Ted caught on and put out his hand in a gesture for her to lead. She took his hand but did not move. Instead, she looked up at him. After another moment, Ted leaned over and picked her up. Myra put her arms around Ted and they walked to the hall. Believing their prayers to be answered, Elizabeth and Oliver looked on at this very warm moment.

Grandma's bedroom was small and crowded with three beds. She was sitting up, leaning on her pillow. Ten-year-old Ruthie sat beside her. A Winchester lever-action rifle was leaning in the corner beside the wise old woman's bed.

Holding Woman, Grandmother to the girls, was speaking to Ruthie, her words loaded with mystique. "No man's name is more distinguished by the Cheyenne than the name of *Mut'si-i-u'iv.*"

Ruthie stumbled through the word. *"Mut'si-u'iv."*

"Mut'si-i-u'iv, the Prophet. Because of his own power and his relationship with the tribe, the Cheyenne called him Sweet Medicine."

Grandmother put out her hand and stopped Ruthie to impart her wisdom. Her speech was labored, but clear and proud.

"Sweet Medicine is also called Eagle's Peak, and sometimes Standing Sweet Grass."

Ted slowly opened the door. Ruthie looked up. Grandma could not see well enough to recognize him, but she sensed Ted's presence.

"Who's there?"

"It's me, Grandma," Myra grinned.

Grandmother knew someone else was there. "But who's with you?"

Ted put Myra down and moved towards Ruthie and Grandma.

"It's Ted, Grandma."

Joy burst across her face and she lit up. "My son. You are home from the wars. Ruthie, your father is home."

Ruthie stood up, not sure what to do. This was more difficult for her. She was old enough to remember her dad, old enough to know her mother's pain, and somehow associated that with her father. There he was, suddenly standing in her bedroom.

Ted reached out, taking his daughter's hand. "Hi, Ruthie."

She took a quick glance up at him but looked over to Grandma for reassurance. Grandmother was, however, so anxious to see Ted that she simply asked, "Come closer, Ted."

He was still holding Ruthie's hand as he leaned down to embrace this beautiful old woman. He loved his grandmother and cherished her face. It spoke volumes about enduring life, as does mother earth.

She could barely make out his features; then her hand reached up to touch him. She pulled him down and he sat on the edge of the bed. In that moment, as her fingers moved across his face, she identified him. "You are your grandfather's son. Sweet Medicine has brought you home to us."

"It's good to be here, Grandma."

Ted continued to hold Ruthie's hand as he leaned back, looking over to her. Myra had stepped close to her sister, not wanting to miss any of this. Ted reached out and took Myra's hand, also. "I am very sorry I've been gone so long. But I'm home now . . . and promise I won't leave you again."

Ruthie just looked. She understood much more than a girl her age should have to.

Myra was quick to pass judgment. "That's good." She had sealed the moment and was ready to move on.

Grandma added, "That is good, Myra. The war is over, right Ted?"

"My war is over." he replied.

But Ted knew that Ruthie really needed a lot more from her father before she would step out from behind her shield. He knew all he could do now was try to convince her. He pulled Ruthie towards him, putting his arms around her. After a moment, face to face, he looked into her big eyes.

"You are very pretty, Ruthie. Just like your mother when she was young."

Ruthie looked at her father, those eyes searching deep inside of him.

Elizabeth came to the door. "Ted, come on, I'll fix you some dinner. We can all visit in the front room."

Without looking away from Ruthie, he responded softly, "I'll be right there, Mom."

He hugged Ruthie again, then let her go. He turned back to Grandma. "You want to come with us, Grandma?"

"No. You go. Come see me when you're done. We'll talk about the war."

"Okay. I'll do that."

"Just tell me, how many of them did you kill?"

He was amused by the seriousness of the question. "I don't know."

"You were in battles. You have to know. It's important."

"Well, I'll have to think about it, and count."

She pointed her strong finger at him. "You must. Now go, eat. We'll talk later."

"Yes, we'll talk later."

Grandmother watched as Ted and the girls left the room. After they had gone she spoke:

"I knew you'd help bring my son home. Thank you."

It was well after dinner and the girls were in bed. Oliver stoked the potbelly while Ted relaxed in one of two wooden rockers pulled up to the warmth of the old stove. Oliver closed the iron door, trapping the flames, and sat back. Ted watched as he picked up his tobacco and paper and rolled a cigarette. This was his dad's evening ritual, and it felt really good to see it again.

"Whenever I see Bull Durham, it always reminds me of you and your after-dinner smoke."

Without reservation, Oliver replied, "Best time of day."

Ted pulled out a cigarette from his pocket as Oliver lit up. "You never got into buying a pack?"

"Nope. Wouldn't be any point to smokin' without rollin' 'em."

A few moments passed.

"How long you had electricity, Dad?"

"'Bout a year, maybe eighteen months now."

"Nice."

Oliver nodded. A few more quiet moments expired.

"So what happened while I was in Denver?"

"Years passed by."

Ted shrugged. "I mean recently."

"The priest called me from the shelter. Told me about your condition."

"I know. He told me you spoke."

Oliver continued with his smoke.

"What's happened with Helen?"

Oliver did not seem to want to answer.

Ted continued, "Why are the girls here?"

"Social Services got the word Helen was drinking all the time. They investigated and took the girls away from her." Oliver added with a little edge. "You surprised? They couldn't find *you*."

There was a certain degree of amazement in Ted. "I never thought it could go that far. When we were together, we drank some."

Oliver leaned forward in disbelief. "Some? Besides fighting, that's all you two did. And when you left for Denver, well, she didn't stop."

"You and Mother, taking care of the girls, I know it's a lot."

Oliver cocked his head. "Do you? Social Services was going to put them in foster homes. Separate them! Fortunately, they listened and we got custody."

A few more moments of silence passed.

"So, what's happened to Helen?"

"She came around a couple of times and visited the girls when she was sober. I think she knows it's better they're with us. Otherwise, haven't seen her for months, Ted."

"Is she still around here?"

"Well. I really don't know." Oliver shifted to a stern voice, one Ted had not heard since he was a kid. "You need to be getting some work, getting back on your feet."

"I know, Dad."

"Why do you want to know where she is?"

"Just wondered."

"You don't need to be looking for trouble. You and Helen are bad medicine."

Ted did not want the lecture.

"You can stay here, sleep on the couch 'til you can get a place of your own."

Ted responded with sincerity. "Thanks."

"Come over to Busby School tomorrow. There's an opening for a janitor. It's steady work during school days. Summers, you can go with the fire fighters."

Ted thought on it for a moment. He had no place for pride in this matter. Work meant money and that was what he needed before he could get back to living.

"Okay, Dad. I'll come over tomorrow."

Oliver studied him for a moment.

"How you doing with the alcohol?"

"I'm all right."

"I don't want to be put in a situation where I've got to explain things about you to the people at school."

"I'm not going to embarrass you."

Oliver took another moment. "Well, no need to talk about thatanymore." He took his last drag and put out the cigarette. "I'm heading to bed."

Oliver got up, paused a moment as he took in the sight of Ted. "Good to have you home, son."

"Good to be here, Dad."

Oliver nodded in agreement and then walked off. Ted watched his dad. He was a proud simple man who lived a quiet and truthful life.

Ted gazed across the room. Photos of the family, his girls with their Grandma, Oliver and Elizabeth on a fishing trip, Grandma proudly holding her trusty Winchester while kneeling beside an eight-point buck, and a photo of Ted in uniform made up the gallery. It was good to be home.

Ted reached to the lamp and turned it off. Moonlight washed in on the room as Ted lit another cigarette. It was good to be home.

CHAPTER 7

JUST SOME BOYS DOIN' THEIR THING

The Busby School was simple. Since it was built of Quonset huts, it had that basic military look. A lone bus was taking on an after-school group of students that ranged in age from seven to sixteen. Oliver was the trusted and reliable driver. He knew every one of the kids by their first name and was ever so patient as they clamored on the bus. With the last student on board and seated, Oliver closed the door and drove away.

Ted was now working at the Busby School. As with all reservation schools, it was run by the Bureau of Indian Affairs, which is a part of the Department of the Interior. Why the schools were not operated under the Department of Education is a question yet to be answered or understood. Who would expect the Department of the Interior to have the personnel with expertise in education? Some political or bureaucratic pundit might wax wise on the subject, giving theoretical justification. Whatever the hypothetical argument, the education of all our citizens belongs under the same department. But this has not been the case for the American Indian children.

A further and more serious complication was the restriction barring the Cheyenne and all other Indian Nations from participation in the education of their children. They were not allowed to participate in any manner, which was completely at odds with their cultural heritage.

Ted was dressed in workman's dark gray. This highly decorated war veteran was found fit enough to push a broom. All of his years as a student in BIA schools were brought to the present as he moved through Busby's halls. There were only three classrooms. The first had a handmade paper sign taped to the door reading *K to 3*. The second door's sign read *4 to 8*. The third door's sign read *9 to 12*.

While he pushed the broom along the corridor towards the administration office, Ted noticed how little things had changed. As he worked his way up the hallway, two members of the faculty walked by, a man and a woman. They were white and very engaged in an argument about women's rights. They passed Ted as if he were a fixture of the building. Another overweight teacher followed who seemed consumed with the need to avoid eye contact with Ted.

A fourteen-year-old girl, a book in hand, was chasing after the overweight teacher, calling out, "Mr. Jones, Mr. Jones." The teacher, as if frightened, ignored the girl while he wrestled with the door to his classroom. Ted watched in disbelief as the teacher escaped to the inner sanctum and locked the door before the girl might reach him. After trying to open the door, she turned with great disappointment and walked past Ted.

Ted, having a good sense of how she might be feeling, asked, "May I help?"

She looked up to him with very disheartened eyes. "I just wanted to return this book."

Ted smiled. "If that's all it is, give it to me and I'll give to him. I'm about to go in there anyway."

The girl seemed a little relieved. "Thanks." She handed him the book and Ted looked it over. It was so worn, Scotch tape was holding it together. The title, *Basic Arithmetic*, was barely readable.

Ted had to comment. "This takes me back. It's the same book I had when I was a student here."

"Is this school that old?" she inquired innocently.

"Afraid so. Hasn't changed much, either."

"Did they have more books then? We have to share these." And she added with exasperation, "That's why I was trying to get it to Mr. Jones."

"Maybe he didn't hear you."

"No. He never answers us. We think he's afraid of us. Well, thanks." She was off as fast as she had arrived.

Ted entered Jones' classroom to find the man eating a sandwich. As if caught stealing, Jones reacted and tried to stuff the food inside his desk drawer. The moment was made even more uncomfortable for Jones as Ted approached him with the book. Ted stood at the edge of the desk with the book in his outstretched hand. Jones was again doing his best to make himself appear to be busy.

Ted finally said, "This is from the student that was calling you. She wanted to return it."

Jones looked out the corner of his eyes but said nothing. Ted finally placed the book on the edge of his desk and added, "I was going to clean the classroom."

Jones said nothing and continued to search through the pages of a book.

Ted watched this pathetic looking man. "You know, it wouldn't hurt you to look at me."

Jones could not do it. Ted backed away. "Maybe I should come back later to clean." Jones nodded approval, almost sighing in relief. As Ted pushed his gear out the door, he thought that the school had changed: The books had gotten older and the teachers worse.

At the end of the corridor, Ted turned to make another pass with the broom. As he swept alongside the glass window to administration, he noticed an attractive Cheyenne woman working behind the counter. Her desk nameplate read *Imogene*.

Ted watched her for as long as he could without being detected. She did not seem to notice him, or so he thought as he continued sweeping. But as he looked away, she watched him and pondered in a fraction of a second what he might be like, this tall quiet man. She wondered if he would have smiled had their eyes met. Her glance was interrupted when the white school administrator, Frank Moore, handed her a file.

Ted pushed his cart and broom into a classroom. Another handmade sign, *9 to 12*, was posted above the chalkboard. The room had thirty very well-worn desks. This was poverty by anyone's standards. But to those living on the reservation, it was the norm.

Ted started work on the floor. As he moved around the room, he began to really notice some of the students' work displayed on the walls, which included papers that appeared to have been written by eight-year-old children, and crayon drawings that would be expected in a third grade classroom.

The door opened and a teacher entered. With light-colored hair and in his late twenties, he seemed incongruous in this place. The teacher moved directly to his desk. As he picked a file from the desk drawer, he noticed Ted and walked over to him, offering a friendly smile.

"I'm Joe Smith, a teacher here. I've only been at Busby about a week. Came here from Bozeman."

Ted just looked at the man. After a moment of silence, he grunted an acknowledgment then moved on with his work.

"Do you speak English?"

Ted stopped and looked back. "Read it and write it, too." He immediately returned to his sweeping.

"I'm sorry. I thought maybe you. . . . "

Ted cut him off. "You thought maybe I was just another dumb-ass Indian? Are you going to talk to your students or just figure they can't speak either?"

Smith turned red with embarrassment and snapped back, "Give me a break, will ya?"

Ted was not the least interested and returned to his work without giving Smith another look. Smith, frustrated, stood for a moment longer, then left.

It was late that afternoon as Ted walked along the edge of the highway. He was feeling the bite of the cold air as the sun began to hide behind a nearby hilltop. The pastureland offered a shorter route to town so he hopped a fence and started across the field. A small cluster of heifers laid well to the north end of the field, enjoying the last of the sun's warmth.

Grandmother's voice returned to Ted's thoughts.

"For our people, the slaughtering of the great buffalo herds was the crime of the many crimes we could never understand. On our grasslands, from time beyond memory, the buffalo had given the Indians of the plains their flesh for food."

The image before Ted changed, and he once again joined in Morning Star's journey. The exhausted, starving, and weather-beaten Cheyenne were continuing their relentless drive towards their homeland. Their ponies now numbered less than fifty. It was late September as the people followed Morning Star and Little Wolf across the field of yellowing grass.

The Cheyenne cleared a slight crest that autumn day and walked into a buffalo hunter's camp. The carcasses of eighteen buffalo, freshly killed and skinned, formed a loose circle around the campsite. Six bearded men, filthy from the hunt, were snoozing around the campfire. They were McCabe, Ward, Anderson, Jones, Lefty, and Cooke, and they were a stinky, raunchy looking bunch. They had filled their bellies with roasted buffalo tongue, biscuits, and whiskey. Asleep, they were oblivious to the advancing threat.

As the Cheyenne approached, they formed a wide circle around the camp. Grandmother's words added to Ted's images as he could only imagine passing the dead animals while starving and being deprived of their land. "The buffalo bones gave weapons and needles, the teeth became ornaments, the sinews thread, the entrails pots and sacks, the hooves glue, and even their droppings fueled the fires.

There was no waste. We killed only what we could use. To us, the herds were the eternal source of sustenance. For no reason could we understand the buffalo hunters killing these herds only for their skin, leaving the rest to rot."

Anderson woke up, reaching for the whiskey jug. To his disbelief, he saw the Cheyenne encircling the camp. He kicked at Ward and stammered. "Wake up! WAKE UP! Indians!"

The others awoke, adrenaline pumping as soon as their eyes focused on what may be their fate facing them, hatred burning in the Cheyenne's eyes. The hunters quickly realized they were surrounded by 300 starving and angry men, women, and children.

The six men got to their feet, McCabe and Anderson each rising with a rifle in hand. But wisely they held them from the breach, letting the muzzles point to the ground.

Ward was beginning to hyperventilate. "Oh God. They're going to kill us."

Anderson hissed. "Shut up, Ward."

"But what are we going to do?" Ward whined.

McCabe added, "If you don't shut up, I'll shoot you myself."

The braves dismounted and moved in, the women and children right behind them. Ward began to cry like a baby. The Indian men watched this and smiled, some with amusement, others with contempt. Pawnee and Wooden Thigh snatched weapons from the men. Some of the women gathered around Anderson and began ripping his shirt off, scratching at him. With that, the braves made a tight circle around the six hunters, locking arms, forcing the women and children back.

As Little Wolf and Morning Star approached, the women stepped aside.

Morning Star spoke to the women. "Take the children. Go prepare food. Some of you break up the wagon for fuel and make a fire for roasting the meat."

The six hostages watched as Little Wolf moved inside the circle, looking them over. He reached in his pocket, pulled out a tobacco pouch, and rolled a cigarette. Morning Star stepped in by his side, slowly, with the regal air of the high Chief. Behind him, other men began breaking up the hunters' wagon and started a fire, while the women were slicing buffalo meat, preparing to cook.

The braves were anxious to act, to avenge the wholesale slaughter of the buffalo. Morning Star's presence may be all that held them at bay.

Although a white hot rage was burning under his skin, Little Wolf talked quietly to Morning Star with much respect. "To our men it is justice to kill these whites."

"To what end?"

Little Wolf felt he needed to remind his old friend. "First came the wagons. Then the Blue Coats to protect them. Then the hunters to slaughter the buffalo and take our food. Then the railroads. Then we were taken to the dry land to die."

As Ward continued to whimper, Little Wolf took note with great disdain.

Morning Star challenged this idea. "And killing these six. How will that help?"

"It will cool the blood. My men want the spirit of the million buffalo that have died like these to know they are not forgotten."

"And this act of revenge will certainly be discovered by our pursuers. Then more Blue Coats will come, and more of our people will die. Is that what we want?" Morning Star asked.

Little Wolf said nothing. He knew there was no argument or justification that would counter Morning Star's logic. After a moment, he stepped to the fire, removed a burning stick, and lit his cigarette. Then he paced, moving around the circle of men. He looked at each one, studying their eyes.

Contemplating, Morning Star watched as Little Wolf continued to smoke. The Cheyenne braves, now chewing on the quickly prepared meat, were anxious for justice. Their wolf-cries rolled over Little Wolf as he walked and deliberated. He finished his smoke and threw the butt in the fire. Then he walked to Morning Star. "What has gone before is gone forever. You are right. There is no justice in this for our children."

Morning Star approved with the slightest nod of his head.

Little Wolf turned to the captives, deliberately, using all his strength to say the words that completely defied his basic instinct: "Leave this place."

The hunters could not believe their ears. Little Wolf repeated the words as the circle of Cheyenne men opened. Without hesitation, the six hunters began running. They ran for their lives, not knowing if this was a game in which they were the prey and would be hunted, run down, and slaughtered like the buffalo. Ward, still crying, ran the fastest. Pawnee and Wooden Thigh chased after them for sport, but ultimately let them get away.

As the men disappeared over the horizon, the Cheyenne women began to pack up what they could of the meat and hides while the braves searched the wagons for ammunition and rifles.

Ted was now at the edge of the field. Town was another two miles down the road. But then, two miles could have been twenty or 200 since Ted was living in an alternate reality that he carried in his blood.

CHAPTER 8
THEIR WIVES

At the main intersection of town, an older pickup truck pulled to the shoulder of the road. Ted stepped out.

"Thanks, buddy."

He walked across the street to the general store and disappeared inside. A few moments later Ted stepped out, opening a fresh pack of Camels. Just as he lit up, his eyes connected with an image that stopped him dead in his tracks. Helen stood a few feet away. She was hollow-eyed as she stared at him. Unconsciously, she straightened her hair when she realized it was Ted.

"Hi, Ted."

Ted took a step towards her while still processing the thought that this person was once his beautiful wife. In a short three steps, he realized that this same women was the mother of his beautiful daughters. How was that possible?

"Helen?"

"When'd you get back?" she asked.

"Couple days ago."

She looked at the freshly lit cigarette and thought it safe to ask, "Got a smoke?"

Ted offered her one, and she took it. He lit it with the Zippo. As he held the lighter, her hand brushed his. At that same moment, their eyes met, briefly.

"How are the girls? I miss them."

Ted backed up one step and replied firmly, "They're lucky to have my parents."

"I know. I'm sorry. So sorry." She inched closer to him.

"So am I." He was not placating her with an admission of responsibility. Ted was living each day in an attempt at restitution for his failure as a parent. "I ain't done much better by them, that's for sure."

"So whatta ya doing here?"

"Just started a job over at Busby."

"You with your dad?"

"I'm staying there for a few days."

She reached out and touched his jacket. "I'm sorry about a lot of stuff."

He looked at her in silence, knowing he did not need to hear this now. Ted could feel that certain thing way inside that Helen brought up in him. Even in this condition, she still rang a bell in him.

She queried him. "Don't you ever miss me? I miss you."

Ted did not know what to say. These words, this meeting, all of it was making him very uncomfortable. "Helen, I gotta get going. You take care of yourself."

Helen grabbed his jacket, stopping him. "I wanna see you."

Ted looked into her eyes. They spoke of desperation more than anything. But there was something else that they offered, something that only Ted would know, something that had been reserved for a time when he knew nothing of tomorrow's mortality.

"Maybe sometime, Helen."

He took her hand off his jacket and walked away.

That night, as was now his custom, Ted sat on the floor watching Myra and Ruthie color in their room. Grandma would sit by the radio, listening to the evening broadcast of the "The Lone Ranger." The familiar voice on the radio announced, "And with a mighty Hi Ho Silver, the Lone Ranger, followed by his faithful companion, Tonto, rides away."

As the theme music played, Grandma looked on at the girls coloring. Elizabeth leaned into the room. "Okay girls, put your drawings away. It's bath time."

Without hesitation, the girls began putting the crayons away.

"Can I get you two anything?" Elizabeth added, "Ted, there's still more pie."

"Thanks, Mother. Not now."

Grandmother looked at her. "We're fine, dear."

Elizabeth smiled at them then went off to the bathroom, the girls following behind. Grandma reached up and turned off the radio.

Ted looked at her with complete disbelief in his eyes. "How do you listen to that, Grandma?"

"I know, I know. Your father asks me the same question."

Ted mockingly imitated the radio announcer. "Tonto, the faithful companion? Why would anyone believe that an

Indian followed some masked cowboy around? The faithful companion," he repeated, shaking his head in disgust.

"Tonto just adapted. Like your great grandfather did. Those days in the stories were when this became white man's land."

Ted shrugged the idea off. But she was quite serious and went on. "It's time for you to figure it out, too. You fought in the white man's army."

"Yes. But not as a second-class citizen."

Grandmother ignored that last comment. She was moving on to something else. Time was too precious to waste on negativity. Ted knew that and suddenly felt like a foolish kid with an attitude. She leaned over to her nightstand, opened a drawer, and removed an old canvas-covered book. Holding it for a moment, she placed the palm of her hand on its cover. Ted watched her. It was clear to him that there were a lot of memories bound to what she held. Then she raised it to her face and smelled the cover. She inhaled deeply so as to take what the book possessed to her deepest cells.

"When you are older, Ted, and your eyes don't work so good, you'll realize more than ever the power of each of your senses. Certain smells take me to other places. Like this book. It carries a story in pictures, but it also brings along a memory with what I smell."

She handed the book to Ted. "Someday you will tell these stories."

The book had frayed edges and was warped from moisture. He sniffed it and tried to recognize what he smelled. "It's a little like sage. Like the high desert after a rain in summer."

Grandmother nodded. "That's some of it."

He opened it carefully, realizing there was a power connected to its legacy. The binding was barely holding the cover together. On the first page was a simple illustration, images of classic native lore, not as primitive as cave drawings. They were in color, almost like pastel chalk.

Grandmother explained. "The time has come for me to pass this on to you. Little Finger Nail made his own record of the Cheyenne Journey. He started me doing the same. This is my diary. I did it when I was alone at Carlisle and surviving on memories."

Ted very carefully turned to a new page. The images were of two Indian men, both wearing headdresses, walking away from each other. Around the edge of the page were images of Blue Coat soldiers and their horses, forming an almost complete circle around the two parting men.

Grandma looked at Ted as he continued to study the sketches.

"Share this with others. They will want to know."

Ted turned another page. The image was of a white and black spotted packhorse and a woman who was loading it. At the perimeter of the image were symbols of the approaching cavalry.

Grandmother went on. "Little Finger Nail was a warrior, but he made games for the small boys; he helped the old women with the horses; sometimes he sang, and he drew our story in his book."

At this point, Ted was lost again in the images of the journey. He could see The Nail that autumn day, sitting a few feet from the other Cheyenne while he drew a scene in his little book. Singing Cloud sat by his side, repairing a hole in his moccasin. Holding Woman watched them from a distance.

The Nail looked on as Bull Hump and Little Hump whooped a small herd of horses out of a hollow. A black mare, spotted in white, and with white eyes, was cut out and offered to Morning Star. He gestured to Short One that she should take the mare. Another horse was offered to Little Wolf for his family. This distracted the warrior Chief from the fire. He was melting lead with some of the braves to pour for new bullets. Little Wolf gestured to Feather on the Head to take the horse.

Very pleased with the gesture from Morning Star, Short One approached the mare, creating a halter from a leather-braided rope she carried. After a few sniffs and a snort, the mare was willing to give herself to the woman and offered her head to the halter. Pawnee Woman's daughters watched, fascinated with this spirited mare. Short One was a mother and teacher to these girls as a part of being a wife to Morning Star.

Just then Pawnee and Wooden Thigh rode in fast and hard through the grass from the south and approached the two Chiefs. Pawnee blurted out. "Blue Coats are coming from the south, Father."

Wooden Thigh added, "And I saw two whites on horseback just over the ridge."

Little Wolf knew there was no time for rest. "We must move faster. More horses for the women and the old ones."

Morning Star sensed something even more important. "Soon we will cross the running water. We will be with our friends and relatives at Red Cloud."

Little Wolf, always the pragmatist, cut into that thought. "Pawnee and Wooden Thigh have seen Crook's army. We may never get to Red Cloud with all the old ones on foot."

Morning Star appreciated the urgency. "We go now. Together! Send them to gather more horses."

Little Wolf turned to Pawnee and Wooden Thigh. "Join with Bull Hump and Little Hump. Go ahead. Find more horses."

Ever cautious about keeping relations with the whites, Morning Star interjected, "Don't kill unless you have no choice. We want no more trouble."

Pawnee and Wooden Thigh turned their ponies and joined up with Bull Hump and Little Hump, charging to the north. They kicked up a dust the breeze blew across the camp.

The Nail, who sketched in his book through this exchange, put away his art and with it that part of him that was a gentle spirit. As a dog soldier with the fearlessness of the wolf, he and Singing Cloud rejoined the others, now readying for travel.

The Cheyenne packed at a frenetic pace. The horses again sensed urgency as they were loaded with bundles. Short One, feeling blessed to have the mare now, tossed her possessions on her pony with the help of her daughters. Its white eyes were widening with every breath. Perhaps it was some danger she anticipated that caused the mare to begin to shy away from Short One.

Then a gust of wind hit as Short One was loading the last bundle on the pony. A dry weed fluttered past the mare and spooked her. Short One, not one to be intimidated by anything, grabbed her by the mane, firmly settling the horse. As she brought the mare into her view, she looked in its now wild eyes and calmly spoke to her with a strength the pony understood.

"Easy my beauty. Together, we will do this."

The flurry of action around the village made all the animals eager to move. Morning Star and Little Wolf, knowing there was no time left, mounted up and started to the north. The others began to fall in line. Short One was lashing the last of the bundles when a rifle shot reported with a ricochet off a nearby rock.

Pawnee Woman immediately turned her attention to her girls. "Stay back until I get on, then I'll help you up."

The girls moved back to the cover of a tree. Grandmother had a very clear image of her mother's fearlessness. At five years of age, Holding Woman believed her mother could do anything.

The Nail, rifle in hand, rode towards the shot to cover his people's departure. The exhausted Cheyenne picked up their pace once again.

Short One's mare was skittish once more. The confident mother grabbed the mare's black mane again to steady her while she attempted to mount the horse. She did this from the right side and slipped her body up, in-between the long leather bundles hanging from the mare. But the horse kept dancing away from her. Short One almost fell.

The eldest daughter, Broken Foot Woman, called out. "Let me help you, Mother. Please."

Perhaps now more than ever, Short One was determined to mount the animal. It was given to her as a help, to carry her things and to carry her daughter. Why would this animal be sent to help her and yet cause so much trouble? Short One firmly pulled on the halter with one hand and took a handful of mane with the other. As she rose up, the horse shied again, this time rearing up. As the mare reared, she dropped her head. This sudden movement caused the long leather bundles to hit the horse's ribs. All the while the determined Short One struggled to hold on. With each second, she became more determined to get herself mounted on the horse.

Broken Foot Woman, now truly fearful, yelled, "Someone help my mother!"

This call turned Morning Star, who immediately saw his wife's jeopardy.

Within that moment the circumstance went from bad to horrible as the mare became completely wild. It reared up high. Short One lost her grip and fell directly under the horse just before its hooves fell to the ground. Short One was instantly crushed under the animal's weight. The mare reared again, turned, and charged away to the north, bucking off the bundles.

Broken Foot Woman and Holding Woman ran to their mother as Morning Star dropped to Short One's side. Ashen faced, this man who had traveled so many roads in his life only to find himself here, took this loyal woman into his arms. Blood ran freely from Short One's mouth on Morning

Star's arm as he cradled her. He gently turned her face to look in her eyes. They showed no life as she took her last breath of air.

The others had rushed in. All that could be done now was to comfort the daughters, who had begun to weep at the sight of their dead mother. Singing Cloud and Feather on the Head held the girls as their father rose with the limp body of their beloved Short One in his arms, Pawnee Woman at his side.

In a solemn voice, he said, "Now Short One belongs to all of you. Even more than before, she is your mother."

Another rifle shot reported, returning an awareness of impending danger. A makeshift travois was rigged behind an old mare, and Morning Star placed Short One's body on it.

The Cheyenne moved on, now led by Little Wolf. A small group on foot followed the body of Short One. They were led by Morning Star, Pawnee Woman, and their daughters.

Grandmother's words brought closure to this moment. "We walked behind my mother, following my father. When a place of safety was reached, we buried Short One. The blood-soaked travois was used to drag stones for her gravesite, stones forever colored in memory of her life. Before leaving, the women gashed their arms and ankles, as they would for a warrior killed in battle."

CHAPTER 9
FALLING OFF

The church hall was crowded with Cheyenne for the monthly Saturday night square dance and social. A poster color paper banner reading *Busby Mennonite Church Saturday Night Social* was tacked over the stage.

The minister visited among the older folks, some sitting at tables playing checkers, others just socializing. Oliver and Elizabeth were among the dancers having a lot of fun. On the stage a pretty good country band played. The caller was having a good time leading the dancers with, "Grab your partner and a dosey doe, around you go."

Ted, the eternal loner, was engaged in dialog with his old friend, Sylvester. They were dipping into the punch bowl and observing the room as the evening went on.

Sylvester was seriously trying to make a point with Ted. "You know there's almost one million bowling lanes in the country now."

Ted was kind of amused. "One million? That's a lot of bowling pins, Sylvester. Takes a lot of trees to make 'em."

Sylvester went on. "Yup. But I'm talking about sports. It's taking over, Ted. That or rock and roll."

As Sylvester spoke, Ted noticed Imogene, who noticed him in return.

"Rock and roll you say. No thanks. I'll stay with Patsy Cline and Hank Williams."

A woman across the room waved at Sylvester, summoning him. He nodded. "See you later, Ted. The war department is calling." Sylvester walked off. Ted looked at Imogene again. She was still standing alone. He grabbed a couple of punch cups and casually drifted across the floor to her. He presented himself with no shyness.

"Hi. I'm Ted." He handed her a cup.

"Thanks. I know who you are."

"Okay. Got me there." He had a cute twinkle in his eye, something that had not happened in many a year. She took a sip of punch. Ted waited patiently, for at least two seconds, before he continued. "Do you have a name?"

"Sure do."

"That's good", he replied. He waited. She took another sip of punch. "You wanna tell me what it is?"

She smiled and said, "Imogene."

"Imogene. Nice name." He thought about it for a moment and nodded another approval. Imogene watched him, wondering what was coming next.

Ted jumped back in, "So how long you worked for those, those people, at Busby School?"

"About two years now, Mr. Rising Sun. And, by the way, I like my job." She handed him back the cup. "Thank you. It was nice to meet you."

Ted watched as Imogene walked away, realizing that he had somehow insulted her. He felt pretty foolish in that moment as he tried to extract his foot from his mouth.

She probably didn't hear him when he said, "Nice to meet you, too." Suddenly he felt as if everyone in the room was looking. He turned away as if searching for something, anything, somewhere in room. As he walked he started a dialog with himself, playing out both sides of a make believe conversation. "So how long you been working with those fools? Oh, Mr. Rising Sun, you're so funny." Then he directed it at himself, "Nice going, idiot. Really good way to start a conversation, knocking the place she works before you even knew what she thought."

Ted pretty much figured his night was over as he drifted around the room. He was becoming increasingly self-conscious, so he headed for the door.

Ted stepped from the hall and lit a cigarette. He was standing next to the parking lot and decided to walk out among the cars. He was admiring a shiny '57 Ford two-door coupe when he heard a bottle hitting the pavement. He looked towards the sound but didn't see anyone. His curiosity was hooked, so he moved in that direction.

Ted stepped between the cars, getting closer to what now sounded like a struggle. He saw a woman fighting off the advances of a man at the open rear door of a sedan.

"Leave me alone!" the woman was pleading.

Ted stepped within view of the car and could see that a man had the woman trapped inside the open door.

"Hey. What's going on?" Ted demanded.

He pulled the man's shoulder and Helen came into view. Ted was shocked. The man, unsteady from booze, took a swing at Ted, catching him on the jaw. It was a lucky swing that knocked Ted off his feet.

The man snarled, "Get outta here." He turned his attention back to Helen, trying to push her into the car. Ted got up, then firmly pulled the man off Helen with one hand. The man took another swing, this one a roundhouse that Ted was more than prepared for. Ted hooked the man with a right to the gut, folding him in two. As he staggered back, coughing and choking, Ted issued a warning. "Stay away from her." Ted gave him the boot, which sent the man staggering off.

Ted turned back to Helen. Her shirt was partly open.

She had been drinking and was having a tough time trying to focus on him. Her words were slurred, kind of thick coming off her tongue. "Is it you, Ted?"

"Yeah. It's me. What are you doing, Helen?"

"You care?"

Ted just looked. It was an overwhelming sight for him. Perhaps he saw himself as he once was, a pathetic drunk. He also saw Helen as a victim of what they had been to each other. All of it wrapped itself around his throat and he had to step back for air. But Helen's legs were giving out. She grabbed Ted as she fell back, taking him with her onto the rear seat, face forward and on top of her.

Ted struggled to back out of the car but Helen was not about to let him go.

"You care about me?"

"You don't know what you're asking me."

Her booze-soaked breath was too much for him. He wanted to turn away but her grip was strong.

"Be with me, Ted, like we used to be."

"Never. I'm not going back to the bottle, Helen."

His eyes were condemning, something that she could not miss, even in her current state.

"You looked at yourself lately?" he asked.

She tried to straighten up. "Oh, I understand. You're not man enough to drink with me."

"Yeah, Helen. I guess that's it."

Ted backed out of the car.

Helen got angry. "You're not a man anymore."

Ted walked away from the car, his pace picking up with each step. Helen yelled, her words following him.

"I need a real man! Like the old days, Ted, when you tried to be a man."

Ted kept walking. He wanted to get far away from those spiteful words and the painful feelings. But he had to move even further from images of the younger, beautiful, and oh-so-dangerous Helen that flashed through his thoughts. Her magnificent body when he first saw her naked. She was stepping out of a lake. Her skin smooth, her body firm, she looked to him to be a goddess. They made love for the first time that same afternoon as the sun set across the water. Then they raced on horseback across a meadow. He could see her laughing face by the warmth of a campfire that night and remembered their promise to each other made under a blanket of stars, to be together as husband and wife. What happened to all that love and desire over time? How cruel a world was this that such absolute beauty, given through the mystery of human emotion and perception, could be destroyed by the same people who shared such a unique bond.

Ted exited the Hardin Liquor Store with a fifth of Wild Turkey in a brown paper bag. He walked around the corner into the shadows of the adjacent alley. The street lamp at the corner cast a shower of light that cut past Ted, leaving only his silhouette stamped out on this cold night. He stood against the building, bottle in hand, motionless. After a moment he opened the bottle, raised it to his mouth, and drank the entire thing.

The bottle now empty, he dropped it. Ted remained still for another moment then stepped forward. He was not out of the alley when his legs buckled and he fell to the ground, face down in a dirty puddle of water.

CHAPTER 10
PARTING

Ted could feel himself falling, as if there were no bottom. He was simply a man sinking through space as the world was passing. Then he began to hear Grandmother's words and see the images of the mouth of a steep, shadowed canyon, as it came into his mind.

Grandmother spoke with pride. "I've heard the newspapers reported that there were thirteen thousand soldiers out to capture us."

At the floor of the canyon the grass was long and inviting. The aspen were just beginning to show signs of fall's approach, some of their leaves golden. The Cheyenne were filing into the protected canyon, exhausted, some barely able to walk. The horses were being turned loose to graze further into the canyon. Pawnee and two Sioux riders approached from the north and greeted the weary people.

Grandmother continued in his thoughts. "After we crossed the Platte River, the air smelled of home. There was a sense among some of us that we were now safe, that since this was our ancient land the soldiers would not take us from it."

Morning Star, Little Wolf, Pawnee, Wooden Thigh, Little Hump, Bull Hump, The Nail, Old Bear, and the two Sioux riders, along with others, counseled around the fire.

Little Wolf wanted hard facts. "So they are taking you from the Yellowstone to the south, where we were taken?"

The younger of the Sioux spoke. "As soon as you are caught."

The older Sioux added. "Nobody wants to go south. But the families are all falling like the trees do when the great wind and fire comes."

The younger Sioux went on. "The Blue Coats let us out to hunt."

Little Wolf wanted more information. "Which troop escorts your people?"

The older Sioux answered. "They are part of the Seventh cavalry."

Little Wolf reacted with a pleased look. "Custer's Army.

They lost many when they attacked Sitting Bull's *Hunkpapa* circle."

Old Bear was alarmed by this. "Ahh-h! I saw that fight. They will kill the helpless ones. They are strong again."

"And White Hat Clark? Our friend. Is he with you?" asked Little Wolf.

The older Sioux answered. "He is with Bear Coat Miles in the Yellowstone. He could not help us. How can he help you?"

Little Wolf put all this together and did not like what it meant. "Then the soldiers are everywhere but none are our friends."

The older Sioux continued. "Yes, they are camped all over the White River country and at Red Cloud."

A long silence fell over the fire. Morning Star, who had only listened, finally rose. His old blanket was in shreds, his grief-stricken face a little red from the warm setting sun.

"We are in *our* land now. Bear Coat Miles has been an honest man."

Little Wolf countered. "They are there for one purpose, to catch and kill us. We can trust no one until we get to the Yellowstone. And then, only White Hat."

Angered by Little Wolf's interruption, Morning Star turned to him. "General Crook was in Red Cloud Agency when we left. He gave us the right to return."

Little Wolf turned dark. "With the whites, we have the right to nothing, unless we hold it in our hand."

The other Cheyenne heard the argument and were circling around to hear their fate.

Morning Star continued with his point. "It is my turn to speak now, my brother. See the death in the faces of our people. You know we cannot last until the Yellowstone. But you say we go there. This is not wise."

Little Wolf took offense. "So, am I the foolish one?"

Many of the younger men began to move in behind Little Wolf in a show of support.

Morning Star wanted no misunderstanding. After coming so far he was not about to let Little Wolf rest on his bruised pride. "No. I said this idea is not wise. We have not enough horses, food. Do you not smell the winter in the air? It will snow before the next moon. We must continue to Red Cloud."

Little Wolf had become adamant. "We must stay together. Only then can we get away. A Cheyenne never caught cannot be killed."

Some of the young men raised their weapons in agreement with Little Wolf, which caused a vocal reaction from those gathered behind Morning Star. Some of the women began to cry, which upset the children. But this was not what Little Wolf wanted at the moment. He turned to the men and raised his hand to silence them.

"I am going north. Those who will follow me, step over here." Little Wolf gestured to his side.

Silence fell as Little Wolf stepped a few feet away from the fire. Then, one by one, led by Pawnee and Wooden Thigh, most of the younger men stepped over to join Little Wolf. His fierce eyes watched Morning Star. The old Chief turned and walked from the council fire. The Nail, Bull Hump, and Little Hump followed Morning Star. The smoke from the campfire grew in intensity, almost casting a fog to lessen the view of each of the two Cheyenne factions.

By morning light a thick white fog had set in. The moment was always difficult for Grandmother to describe. Her words choked as her throat would become very dry. "And so it happened. We were split in half. And by the rising of the sun, Morning Star and his followers were gone."

Early that morning Little Wolf stepped through the fog to discover that his old friend was gone. Then he discovered a treasure left in a gesture of goodwill. A tattered buffalo robe was placed like an offering with a small mound of ammunition and some powder. Little Wolf realized that Morning Star had given much of what little he had to defend himself. Morning Star, as always, was a great Chief. Little Wolf looked on at the offering and honored the moment in his thoughts.

As Little Wolf made his discovery, Morning Star was standing at the head of a single file of his followers at the top of the canyon. Grandmother, his youngest daughter who was nearing her sixth birthday and who had known nothing but strife, and now the death of Short One, stood at her father's side. She was cold, hungry, and like all of the Cheyenne, exhausted beyond imagination.

A sparrow fluttered near them as it picked insects off a tree limb. Morning Star noticed his little girl, Holding Woman, looking at the bird. "My daughter, that little bird works hard. It will never give in to snow, wind, rain, or the summer sun and the heat it brings. The bird will work to feed its family and live another day."

He looked at her, wanting her to understand. He continued. "Learn from that little bird's courage."

She understood and answered. "Yes, Father."

The sunlight began to cut through the morning fog. Morning Star saw the path and began the final leg of their trek home.

Oliver was standing with a young white doctor in a hospital corridor, looking through the door's window at Ted.

"Alcohol is poison for him," the doctor commented.

"He knows."

"But to drink a whole bottle? What could he be thinking?"

"He wasn't. Maybe there are just times when you don't want to hear your thoughts, the painful memories of war.

"Vets, post traumatic stress syndrome. Rapid consumption of large quantities of alcohol. Never seen it this bad."

"If you wanted to drink and it was illegal for you to have it in your home, what would you do?"

The doctor looked at Oliver for the answer.

Oliver explained. "Indians drink the liquor as soon as they get it, then there's no worry about being arrested for possession."

The doctor turned his look towards Ted.

Oliver continued. "Life's a little harder on some folks, doctor. That's not an excuse. It's simply the truth."

Ted was tied into the bed, writhing in pain from the alcohol poisoning. There were deep lines in his face, beads of sweat running through them. Only he could hear Grandmother as she continued taking him on the journey.

"To some, your great grandfather seemed the fool. They called him the white man's wife because he wanted the children to learn the way of the whites. But he had long ago learned to trust in his own thoughts, to not listen to voices that did not understand the changing world we lived in."

CHAPTER 11
FATE

Everything was white. Imagine opening your eyes to pure white. No shadows, no color, pure white. At first Ted wondered if he was breathing; was he alive or was he now beginning to see the afterlife? Then he heard the door open and a figure, dressed in white, was above him. Ted did not quite make out what was being said but somewhere in his consciousness he realized that this was a nurse and he must be in a hospital. He could barely feel the needle being inserted in his vein. What would they be giving him? Before he could even speculate, the nurse was gone.

Somewhere in all that his mind was carried by the spirit within him to another kind of white. This was one wrapped in a cold wind that brought with it the threat of snow. It cut through Morning Star and his now 150 followers as they pushed on for the northwest.

In a scattering of columns, the younger men scouted in the forward positions on the few healthy ponies. The children and the very old rode on the weaker of the horses, and those that could, walked.

The wind was kicking up the sand, making each step of the trek almost unbearable. To most anyone else it would have been impossible.

It was October 23, 1878. Morning Star and his followers were near Chadron Creek, Nebraska. The blowing dust and sand were moving like waves across the rolling hills. The rags the Cheyenne were wearing trailed from their bodies like ribbons. With many of their people barefooted now, they moved in an almost ghostlike manner, as slowly as imaginable, short of standing still.

Morning Star still carried himself with dignity. He led his people from the center column and was flanked by his sons and The Nail. The sun was dropping on the horizon, casting an orange light and fingers of long shadows that lay in their path.

As the Cheyenne continued against the wind, silhouetted phantom images of soldiers begin to reveal themselves in and out of the windswept and sunbathed horizon. Morning Star strained to see. The young warriors were seeing the same images. Morning Star stopped. The few young braves formed a protective semicircle from his sides as the view became clear. The Cheyenne had walked into a detachment of U.S. Cavalry.

Captain J. B. Johnson, the commander, sat motionless in his saddle looking at this unbelievable sight. To his right 2nd Lieutenant George Chase strained to understand what he was seeing.

Chase finally asked, "What is it, sir?"

"Quiet, Lieutenant," the Captain responded.

Through the dust and sand, the ghastly sight of this exhausted band of 150 Cheyenne revealed themselves. Hollow-eyed, hollow-cheeked, barely able to remain upright, their black hair was hanging loose in the wind. Yet, there was an evident sense of pride and honor. The braves were armed, some with rifles in hand, others with bows or lances.

Chase could not believe the sight. "That's what we've been hunting?"

Johnson turned to him. "Yes Lieutenant, those must be the fierce Cheyenne dog soldiers that evaded everyone until now."

Up and down the line of mounted cavalry the look was the same: total disbelief of this macabre scene, the caricatures of what had once been "the beautiful people."

Johnson continued to express his reaction to this absurd sight. "Twelve thousand men of the armies of the plains have been pursuing these people from the Indian Territories through Kansas, and on to Nebraska, and we are the ones who capture them. What justice is there in this?"

Chase naively asked, "You don't think they'll put up a fight, do you, sir?"

"When people have come this far and paid such a price, it wouldn't take much for them to squeeze a trigger, Chase."

"I understand, sir."

The officers looked on for another moment.

Johnson changed his tone. "Call the quartermaster."

Chase turned and called a soldier nearby. "Sergeant Allen, report to the Captain."

Allen walked his horse up to Captain Johnson and saluted. Johnson returned the salute.

"Allen, bring me some hardtack and meat."

"Yes, sir."

Allen turned back to the packhorses and retrieved a pair of bags.

"I cannot let something insane happen here, for history to record." Johnson was speaking more to himself than to Chase.

Allen returned and handed the bags to Johnson. Johnson turned to Chase. "Hold the men here. Do nothing that shows aggression."

"Yes, sir." Chase responded with an eagerness to obey his superior to the letter.

Johnson gently kicked and his horse moved forward. He slowly advanced, closing the distance to the Cheyenne. He held the reins in his left hand, the bags of provisions in his right. Feeling alone, Johnson stopped about twenty feet from the Cheyenne. He took in the arc of twenty braves prepared to protect their families. His eyes settled on Morning Star who watched him with steady eyes. With the flat of his hand, the Chief firmly gestured to his men for calmness.

Cautiously and with deliberate movement, Johnson dismounted.

He took a few steps towards Morning Star but stopped when he heard the click of The Nail's rifle hammer being cocked. Johnson slowly placed the bags on the ground. He opened them to expose the contents to the Cheyenne. He placed a few of the hard biscuits into view, then stood upright. With a gesture, he offered the food.

"For your people."

He waited but there was no response. After a few moments, he tried to communicate again, not having any clue whether they understood.

"*Sabe* English? Surrender. You are surrounded."

Johnson gestured to his company of cavalry, a strong contrast to the starving Cheyenne. But there was only more silence.

"Surrender. We'll give you more food, and water."

There was no gesture, not the slightest movement from the Cheyenne. Johnson slowly turned and took the reins to walk his horse back to his waiting troops.

He had taken three steps when he heard the words from Morning Star. "Go away."

Johnson cautiously turned in disbelief.

"We want to go home. Let us pass," the Chief added.

Johnson, with a true sadness, shook his head. "I can't do that, Chief."

"Not want fight. We want to go home."

"I understand. But you must surrender. Please don't force my hand. Your people will die."

The sun was rapidly setting. All Johnson could see and hear was the great resolve in the eyes and voice of Morning Star.

Morning Star responded, "We are already dead unless we find our way home. Go away." After a few more moments, Johnson realized that this was not the moment when he should demand anything of these desperate people.

"You take the food. I am going back to my men. We camp there,you camp here. We'll work this out in the morning."

Morning Star said nothing. Johnson turned and walked his horse back to his men.

Grandmother's voice was veiled in Ted's thoughts. "Morning Star knew that to keep us alive he had no choice but to accept the offer of the Blue Coats. The next day we surrendered to the promise that we'd be given shelter and food at Fort Robinson. The great white father in Washington would be asked permission for us to continue to our home, as it had been promised. Forty-four days and seven-hundred-fifty miles had passed since we left the Indian Territory."

It was a cold afternoon as Oliver drove Ted home from the hospital. Ted looked drawn from his days in recovery. They had driven for miles before Oliver spoke.

"Your girls missed you."

"I missed them."

Oliver did not accept that easy response. "It's not that simple, Ted."

"I know."

"No, you don't know. You broke a promise to them. Myra will be happy to see you, but Ruthie, she's old enough to be angry with you. And she has good cause."

Ted lit a cigarette, coughing as he inhaled.

"You broke a promise to me. The school thinks you were in the hospital because of a war injury." Oliver thought for a moment then added, "I guess that's not all a lie."

"Thanks for covering."

"I don't like to think of it that way." Oliver was frustrated. By his way of thinking, this did not need to be happening. Ted could be living his life without destroying himself. But this was not the time for a speech about self-destructive behavior.

They rounded a bend, passing a farmer's growing junk-yard of old vehicles. Maybe it was the time for Ted to participate in a Cheyenne ritual dance that would help him clean out whatever might be lingering in his thoughts from the war.

Oliver started, "Son." He stopped himself. Ted looked over, waiting for his dad to continue. Oliver glanced at Ted, wondering if he was ready for this experience. After a moment, he decided it was the right thing for his son.

Oliver continued, "The time has come for you to do the enemy dance. Clean these things from your head, your memory of the war, the anger about being an Indian in a white man's world. Get on with life."

"You don't know what I feel."

Oliver once again would not accept this from Ted. "I've been here, long before you. I know what it's like in this world. I was in the service. I've been on both sides of this thing. I've also been a dad and a grandfather. And I know your family needs you, *now*. Rise to the occasion of your life or you will live in the shadows forever."

Oliver stopped with the dialog. He was a man of few words. Ted knew to listen, however. When his dad had something to say, Ted listened. But the speech was over as quickly as it had begun. As they rolled on towards home, Ted was left to think.

The pickup settled to a stop in front of Oliver's house. As Ted stepped from the truck, Myra ran out the door and greeted him happily. Ruthie, however, stood on the steps, Elizabeth one step behind her. Ted, with Myra in hand, walked up the steps to the porch. He knelt in front of Ruthie. After a moment he reached out and hugged her. Oliver watched from the base of the steps, Elizabeth from above them. As parents, they could only pray that their son had reached a turning point.

Ted searched Ruthie's eyes, wanting to see whether she could forgive him. As he did, this veteran of two wars, highly decorated soldier, combat experienced and tough man, began to cry. He was in control of everything but his eyes. They told Ruthie the unmistakable truth about her father. He was truly ashamed that he had failed her in his promise. He could not say the words again. This time it was not necessary. As the tears streamed down his face, his eyes said it all to both girls.

As he knelt with an arm around each of them, Ted made a silent promise to *Maheo*. The Great Mystery had given him back his family. Ted Rising Sun would dedicate the rest of his life to his children, but even further, to all the children of the Cheyenne.

Later Grandmother explained to Ted what the enemy dance would do. "The enemy dance will release the spirits of those you killed in the war. That is why I asked you how many enemy you killed in battle. You must write the words to a song that will tell this story. You must make your dance tell of your actions in battle up to the moment of taking the enemy life. And then, in front of someone who is a living witness to your story, you will dance to reenact the moment when you killed the enemy. Only then will you free the spirit."

This is a tradition of the Cheyenne. Had Ted been schooled by his people rather than the BIA, he would have known of this. But such tradition was lost to his generation until the grandmothers were allowed to speak of it.

CHAPTER 12
ENEMY DANCE

Fires of this size seem to reach the heavens, their embers leaving the rising licks of flame, elevating to join the stars. The center point of such a nighttime ceremony as this one for Ted Rising Sun was the fire. The drums and flute created yet another essential element, melding with voices of a group of Cheyenne who sang the lyrics of Ted's story.

The participants were many and included Oliver, Elizabeth, Ruthie, Myra, Grandma, and the very important witness to Ted's war experience, Corporal Kowalski, who was dressed in uniform. Imogene was also among the spectators.

They all sat to observe as Ted, outfitted in ceremonial dress, danced around the huge fire. Hanging from a lodge pole braced near the fire was a piece of hide with the shape of a man painted in white.

The drum rhythm accented by the flute aroused a deep animus in Ted, while the chanting of the story wove an individual meaning to be understood by those present. As he began to move through his reenactment, Ted was finding himself transformed by some mystical power overtaking his mind and body. His dance became more potent, and he was no longer in control of his body. Those watching were feeling the transformation as well. Somewhere within it all, Ted sensed leaving his body. As with the rising embers, he was moving through time.

The unfolding story told through those chanted lyrics brought Ted to the juncture when he took up the ceremonial spear and prepared himself for the kill. The tale being recounted by the singers took Ted through the moments when his comrades were shot by that invisible enemy, when with great intensity he searched the wall of dense trees for the faceless opponent who killed from the darkness.

Ted's eyes scanned the entire perimeter of the ceremonial circle. All there encountered him in that sweeping search for an enemy. Then he locked his focus on the symbol of the man painted on the hide. In slow motion Ted brought the spear to the ready, then cocked his arm as if it were strung like a powerful crossbow. In a half rotation of his arm, he sent the spear on a deadly flat arc to its target. The spear lanced the image of the man directly on the heart.

At that moment, everything stopped. Ted dropped to his knees feeling the emotion release that he had contained for so many years. Corporal Kowalski stood and walked to Ted. Standing over him, he loudly and proudly exclaimed, "And this is how it happened. I was there in North Korea. In this act, Ted, High Hawk, Rising Sun saved my life in battle."

Kowalski reached out to Ted, giving him his hand. As Ted rose, the ceremonial drums picked up their rhythm and other dancers began to move about the fire. Ted looked up at the rising sparks from the fire following their spiral into the blackness of the night with his eyes.

Grandmother had given Ted the image of the ceremonial dance that November of 1878, when the Sioux honored their Cheyenne brothers at Fort Robinson after their capture at Chadron Creek. This was Nebraska Territory and the Cheyenne were not far from their ancestral land. The Sioux lived not far from this place at the Red Cloud Reservation.

The Cheyenne were wearing new blankets and were recovering from their forty-four day ordeal. Lieutenant Chase and Captain Johnson watched from just inside the door as the visiting Sioux passed out moccasins to the Cheyenne.

Chase was pleased. "It certainly ended well."

"For the moment, George. Fate brought them here, but Washington will decide their future." Johnson had his doubts about the kindness these people might expect.

For the moment, though, the relief on the faces of the mothers, their men and children warm and fed, made for a warm sight. Chase took particular pleasure in handing out sour balls to the young Cheyenne. Those very wise children had now figured out that the lieutenant was an easy mark for sweets.

Outside, the ground was a blanket of white. It had been snowing for many days.

Christmas Eve is a night generally reserved for the warmth of family, a deep sense of commitment to one's religion, and certainly a night to act in a "Christian" manner. Captain Henry W. Wessells, Jr., Fort Robinson's newly appointed commander, addressed Captain Johnson from behind his desk. Wessells was a little man. He typically found a way to exercise his authority, particularly with officers who were tall, strong, and proud. Johnson carried all the right qualities and was most certainly envied by Wessells.

"Captain Johnson, General Sheridan's position is quite clear."

Wessells picked up a telegraph paper. He read out loud. "Unless these Indians are sent back, the reservation system will receive a shock which will endanger its stability. If Indians can leave without punishment, they will not stay on reservations." Then he looked up at Johnson and said, "As soon as arrangements are concluded, they are going south. Meanwhile, you will join with Colonel Carlton's Third Cavalry in pursuit of Little Wolf and the rest of the renegade Cheyenne."

Seeking Johnson's agreement and approval, Wessells could not help but notice the captain's hesitation.

Wessells asked, "What is it?"

Johnson offered a valid point. "Having given so much to reach this place, I find it hard to imagine that Morning Star will agree to your terms."

"What choice will he have? They surrendered all their weapons, right?"

Not sure of the answer, Johnson slowly shook his head.

At that moment, Lieutenant Chase opened the door.

Chase blurted out, "I've got the Chief here, sir."

Wessells sat up straight. "Bring him in, Lieutenant."

As Chase stepped away, Wessells turned back to Johnson and confidently added, "We'll soon find out."

Morning Star entered, followed by Chase. The Chief was elegant in his movements as he nodded to Johnson. Morning

Star had an instinct about Johnson that developed from their fateful meeting at Chadron Creek. He was an officer who could be trusted.

"Chief, have a seat." Wessells was being as officious as he was short. Morning Star took a chair next to Johnson. Chase remained standing.

Wessells dove right in. "We have received word from Washington. You and your people are to be returned to the south, to the Indian Territories where you belong."

Morning Star turned to Johnson.

"Is this true? The word of the great father?" Morning Star purposely had asked Johnson. He had to know the truth before returning to the others.

Johnson very frankly but kindly answered. "Yes sir, I believe it is."

Wessells took offense. "Captain Johnson is no longer in charge of your people. In fact, he leaves tomorrow with the Third Cavalry to capture Little Wolf and the others."

Morning Star stood and turned his attention to Wessells. The tired old leader of the Cheyenne made his point very firmly. "The land to the north is the home of the Cheyenne. Our fathers are buried there. Our children were born there."

Wessells was totally unaffected. "This is not open for negotiation. You go tell your people to prepare." Wessells turned his eyes away from Morning Star. He was intimidated by the Chief and certainly, somewhere within all his cold-blooded behavior, one would hope that he knew this was a gross injustice.

Morning Star had not broken his look at Wessells. "Many things we have been asked, and the Cheyenne have done.

But to this I say no. We will not leave our land again." He turned to Johnson. "Thank you for your kindness."

Morning Star did not wait for a reply from Wessells. He turned to the door and was gone. Chase, speechless, went after him. Wessells, totally surprised by Morning Star's decisive reaction, felt the Chief's word was a challenge to his authority.

Wessells mouthed off in the privacy and safety of his office, "We'll test that resolve with a little starvation, thirst, and cold. Crying children will change those words. He will come back and beg."

Johnson, feeling contempt, held nothing back. "You can't be serious."

Wessells, now feeling Johnson's lack of approval, responded firmly, "More than you can imagine. But you won't be here to find out just how serious a man I am."

CHAPTER 13
ONE LISTENED

A classroom turns silent when the students are gone. Yet there is a life that speaks through the displays so often found on walls or even more so, from the leftover chalkboard notes. A teacher has used that black slate surface and a piece of white chalk to bring emphasis to a subject, to drive a point into the minds of pupils. Those writings, scribbles, formulas, notes, examples, or quotes generally carry the seed to whatever lesson has been placed before the class to consume, digest, discuss, and ultimately gain understanding.

Ted pushed his cleaning equipment into the 9 to 12 classroom. Before he began his routine, he admired the Christmas tree that sat near the teacher's desk. The tree looked cold, though, sitting in the unlit room. So Ted found the light cord and plugged it in. The tree came to life, as did the rest of the room. Ted took close notice of the handmade decorations on the tree as well as those hanging around the room.

At first he missed the note on the chalkboard reading *JAN-ITOR, PLEASE WASH.* But then he read the instruction and the words to be erased.

MIDDLE-CLASS AMERICAN VALUES.

RIGHTS. LAND OWNERSHIP.

RESPONSIBILITIES. PROPERTY TAXES.
DISCUSSION TOMORROW. READ PGS 245-250.

Ted commented to himself. "Rights. Land ownership."

He picked up the eraser and wiped through the words. With the board clean, he picked up a piece of chalk and began to write. It was as if a stream of consciousness was flowing through his fingers. When he finished his words, he did not read them but simply put down the chalk and went back to his duties, cleaning the room. When finished, he unplugged the Christmas tree lights and pushed his cart to the next room, leaving these words to greet the next reader:

Once, only Indians lived on this land. Then came strangers from across the Great Water. No land had they; we gave them our land. No food had they; we gave them of our corn. The strangers became many and now they fill all the country. They dig gold from our mountains; they build houses with the trees from our forests; they make clothes from the hides of our animals. None of the things that make their riches did they bring with them from beyond the Great Water. All this comes from the land that the Great Mystery gave to the Indian.

The following day, in front of a full class of students, Joe Smith read Ted's words out loud. He was affected by the power of their meaning. The last paragraph struck him deeply.

And when I think upon this, I know that it is right, even this. In the heart of the Great Mystery it was meant that strangers/visitors, our friends across the Great Water, should come to our land; that I should bid them welcome; that all men should sit down with me and eat together of my corn. It was meant by the Great Mystery that the Indian should give to all people.

Smith stood for several moments in silence. Then he turned to the class. "Do any of you know who wrote this?"

Not having the answer, the class was silent.

The school day being over, the halls were quiet that afternoon. Ted pushed a broom along the floor as he passed empty classrooms. As he swept past the 9 to 12 classroom, Joe Smith opened the door.

Smith approached Ted cautiously. "Excuse me."

Ted stopped his work and looked at Smith.

Smith continued. "We met a few weeks ago."

"Yes. I remember."

"Would you step in for a moment, please?" Smith was very gracious.

Ted nodded, put down the broom, and followed Smith into the classroom.

Smith walked to the chalkboard. Ted's writing was still evident.

"I want to introduce myself again, I'm. . . . "

Ted politely cut him off. "Joe Smith. From Bozeman, right?"

"Right. And you are?"

"Ted Rising Sun. From Busby."

Smith put out his hand and they shook.

Then the teacher inquired, "By any chance, did you write this?" He gestured to the chalkboard.

"Yes. Not a problem, is it?"

"A problem? Quite the contrary, Mr. Rising Sun. It's amazing. It made me feel rather strange about the lesson I was teaching the students."

Ted decided to explain. "To the Cheyenne way of thinking, owning what was given to us by grandmother earth, or the Great Mystery, is a strange concept. We belong to the land, we don't own the land."

Smith, perhaps now getting his first true sense of the culture of the people he was teaching, spoke in genuine amazement. "What an unusual, but wonderful idea. I can't think of how I'd argue the point."

Ted agreed with a nod. "It's really about a respect for the land."

Lights were turning on in Smith's mind. "Would you mind, could you maybe come in early one of these days and speak to the students?"

"Speak about what?"

Smith was inventing, for the idea was so fresh. "The Cheyenne philosophy you've been taught would be very instructive. For me, especially."

"I'm surprised to be asked."

"Why?"

Ted looked carefully at this stranger. Then he decided the man's interest was real. "You know what it was like when I went to school here? We were onlyallowed to see our parents on Saturdays or a holiday. The last thing the BIA wanted was for any of our culture and traditions to be taught."

"Well, certainly that's changed." Smith blurted. "I can only see good in it. So, how about next Wednesday?"

"Okay. Sure you don't want to check with the office first?"

Smith, with confidence, put out his hand. "I'll see you here Wednesday."

They shook warmly. Ted started for the hallway but turned back. "Why are you here?"

Smith did not understand and had no idea how to answer the question.

Ted explained. "The BIA doesn't hire teachers like you. They can't find teachers like you. Why are you here?"

Smith smiled. "My mother asked me the same question. She couldn't understand why I'd give up the country club membership she had given me when I graduated." He shook his head slightly. "It's what I want to do. Teach kids who will listen."

As Ted pushed the broom down the hall, a grin spread across his face. He could hear those familiar words from Grandmother.

"Someday they will ask. And you will tell them our story."

For the first time, Ted agreed. "I will, Grandma. I found someone who wants to listen."

Christmas 1878 had arrived, and with it more snow. The compound in front of the prison barracks was dotted with freezing sentries doing their best to keep hands and feet warm. There were guards posted at each corner of the building. The main doorway was chained closed.

From within the barracks, the sound of wood breaking could be heard. It was the only sound on that still night as Lieutenant Chase approached Sergeant Biglasky at the main door.

"Sergeant, what is going on in there?"

"They're breaking up benches to fuel their stove, Lieutenant." The sergeant added, "Can't exactly blame the poor bastards. It's freezing. Hell of a thing on Christmas."

"Open the door," the lieutenant ordered.

Biglasky turned to Private Janzohn, who stood in front of the door.

"Janzohn, open the door for the lieutenant."

"Right away, Sergeant," Janzohn blurted.

Janzohn, his fingers in pain from the cold, struggled with the cold lock. Freeing the chain, he pulled it clear of the door, then opened it.

Chase entered the barracks. Biglasky and Janzohn stood by the door looking on at the lieutenant.

Chase stepped a few feet into the room. The wood from a broken up bench sat beside the potbelly. Flames licked the outside of the iron door. The women and children were huddled near the heat. Their desperate eyes followed Chase as he stepped closer.

Morning Star stepped from a group of men that included The Nail, Little Hump, and Bull Hump. He approached Chase.

"We must die like this? The great white father wants this to be so?"

The young lieutenant was in deep turmoil. His sense of morality was at odds with his sense of military duty. "No. Please. Chief, let us take the children out and feed them."

Morning Star looked on at the children and the women.

A thoughtful moment passed. "I did not lead my people here, they did not fight to get themselves all the way to our home, just to give up. We live as one, we die as one."

"You understand that Captain Wessells will allow you no more food?"

"And soon we will have no wood."

Chase was frustrated and pained by the suffering.

"I don't know what more to say. I don't understand any of this." Chase turned and walked from the room. As Janzohn locked the door, Chase spoke to Sergeant Biglasky.

"This is craziness."

"Sir, are we really going to starve these people to death?"

"Everyone believes they'll give in. That old man isn't going to give in." Chase uttered this hopeless reply before walking off.

Ted was sitting on the edge of Smith's desk telling this story of Christmas 1878 to the class.

"My grandma was there as a young girl. Younger than any of you."

The school administrator, Frank Moore, and Imogene stood in the rear with Smith. Most of the students were riveted by the way Ted was telling a story that many had probably already heard.

Ted gave them some background. "The women had been put to work unloading supply wagons for the military and had hidden small amounts of grain in their pockets. Those hidden bits of rice were all they had left. That and time. How much time 'til they were starved to death?"

Ted noticed a teenage boy looking at the wall clock, apparently becoming bored with the story. Ted approached him.

"Got an important date?" Ted asked.

The boy was embarrassed. "No."

"Time pretty important to you?"

"Yeah, sometimes it is."

"It's okay. If I were you, I'd be looking at the clock, too."

A little nervous laughter relieved the moment. Moore, however, was not amused by any of this. Ted returned to the front of the room.

"The white man brought us the concept of the clock. Now, everything is done by the clock. We eat to it, sleep to it, you go home and it tells you when to listen to your favorite radio show. I come to work by it. You go to school by it."

A little more laughter of agreement filled the room.

Ted continued. "And eighty years ago, Morning Star knew his people had to accept what time had changed. He believed there was a future for his people, you and me. He also knew the children should be schooled in the ways of the white man's world. So the next time Mr. Smith puts up some boring assignment, you remember that not so long ago your ancestors walked for forty-four days to come home to what had been their land. They were willing to die so we could have a place to call our home."

Ted looked around the room. The students' eyes were glued to him.

Smith asked, "But what happened at Fort Robinson?"

Ted found this a great opportunity to pass on a challenge. "Which one of you would like to finish the story so your teacher will learn?"

Several hands were raised. As this happened, Moore left the room.

It was later that afternoon when Ted entered the main building, pushing the trash cart. His session with the students had brought a fresh light to his day as well as theirs. He was remembering the wonder of their faces, how terrific he felt as he had talked with them. Maybe things were changing.

Ted passed the administration office as Moore and Smith were arguing within view of Imogene. As Ted and Imogene exchanged a quick look, Moore noticed Ted. He called out, but Ted did not hear him.

A few feet down the corridor Moore caught up with Ted.

"Mr. Rising Sun, we need to talk."

"Okay." Ted responded with curiosity, turning halfway towards the man.

"You probably know I'm the superintendent of this school. My name is Frank Moore."

"Yes."

"We have a very precise curriculum. I have just explained to Mr. Smith that it is imperative that he follow our established practices and class guidelines. That does not include lectures on the myths of your Indian history. The students don't teach us, Mr. Rising Sun, we teach them. And, we have textbooks that adequately present American history."

Ted was not taking well to the tone of this proclamation. He responded quickly. "Those would probably be the same textbooks given when I attended here."

"I'm sure they've been updated."

Ted faced him straight on. "You know, I left here before my senior year and hitchhiked to Kansas so that I could enroll in a parochial school, a Mennonite academy. And a funny thing happened when I got there. Got any ideas what that might have been?"

Moore was clueless.

Ted continued. "I couldn't pass the entrance exam. I had to enroll as a freshman. I was seventeen, a senior here, a product of this school, and I knew less than the freshman kids at the Mennonite academy. So, I wouldn't be too sure about your curriculum. But I will tell you, get more teachers who care, like Joe Smith."

Ted shoved the broom into Moore's hands. As he walked on, he passed Smith and stopped to shake his hand.

"It was a pleasure speaking to your class, Mr. Smith. Thank you for your interest. I wish there were more like you."

Ted then walked out the door.

Outside, Imogene ran after him, calling, "Mr. Rising Sun."

He turned as she caught up to him.

She continued. "What you did today, with the class, that was wonderful."

Ted thought differently. "Wonderful? I don't know. For that one moment, when I felt all their eyes on me, that was good."

Imogene was too excited for humility. "It was more than good."

Ted had begun looking around the campus. "In my day, this place had a dairy we worked in. There were no day students.

The buildings were rickety then. So the BIA rebuilt it with army surplus, but nothing has changed. For a minute today, I thought it had."

He looked at her for a moment, taking in her sincerity, then replied, "Thanks for walking out here."

After a moment he walked on.

Imogene called out to him. "Are you going to the Saturday dance?"

He stopped and turned. "Hadn't thought about it. Maybe."

"Good. Maybe I'll see you there."

Ted shrugged his shoulders. "Maybe yes. Maybe no."

He walked off with a playful attitude to his step.

CHAPTER 14
FLIGHT TO FREEDOM

"As a child, the world, your survival, are in the trust of your mother and father. At five I knew only war, imprisonment, starvation, and death." Grandmother said, looking at Ted. Her eyes could make out the image of the person, but no features.

"I don't know how any of you survived. Not just because of starvation and cold but because what hope did you have? After coming so far to be told you must return to the place where so many of you died, how could you have any spirit?"

Grandmother continued with her story. "For the children, they trusted in their parents. It was painful for mothers to listen to the cries of hunger, to see the bloated bellies of their children. My mother was spared this sight. My sister and I stayed huddled together for warmth."

As Ted listened, the images once again took life within his thoughts. It was January 9, 1879. The windows in the barracks were covered with blankets from the inside. In the center of the room, the floorboards had been ripped up. Some of the planks had been fashioned into clubs, smaller pieces were being burnt for warmth, and large sections were barricading the door.

The Nail, Bull Hump, and Little Hump removed a cache of rifle parts that the Cheyenne had hidden under the floorboards. The men, with help from the women, assembled the five rifles and three pistols they had hidden. The women handed Morning Star the little ammunition they managed to hide in their necklaces.

Grandmother's voice punctuated the urgency of the situation. "On some, the mask of death was showing. The Nail chanted a song that filled the room with the wish we all had."

Help me, Posers of the wind and the
sky. And the earth in the cold
nighttime. Help me get my people away.

Outside, a light snow was falling. The sentries were posted at the corners of the building. A scant amount of light showed through the blankets that covered the prison barracks windows. It was a strange scene compounded all the more by the stillness in the air.

Wessells nervously approached Lieutenant Chase and Sergeant Biglasky. "Did your men eat, Lieutenant?"

"They did not seem very hungry, sir."

Wessells inquired further. "Was it your idea to have the mess sergeant ask me what to do with all the leftover food from tonight's meal?"

"No, sir."

Wessells turned and took a step.

Chase added a thought. "I might suggest an idea, sir."

Wessells spun around. "If I want a suggestion, Lieutenant, then you will have an opportunity to tell me."

Wessells was almost baiting Chase. He added, "I want Morning Star put in chains. And any of the braves that try to interfere."

Chase calmly stated, "We can't get in the barracks, sir."

"What do you mean?" the Captain asked.

"They've barricaded us out."

Wessells became flustered. "How can they do that? We locked them in!"

Chase did not have an answer; neither did Biglasky, who merely shrugged. The chanting from within the barracks then got Wessells' attention. "What is that?"

Chase explained. "They sound different tonight, sir. I don't know what it means."

Biglasky added. "If I may, sir. Starvation is taking them over the edge."

Wessells paced, truly perplexed. He had no authority left. Then, a strange grin came over his face. It was as if he had found redemption in a thought. "Well, what can they do? They have no weapons, right?"

Chase just looked at the captain, truly not knowing what to think. "It must be pretty bad in there."

Wessells acted out from his concept of rank. "Losing your nerve, Lieutenant?"

"No, sir. It just has to be desperate for them. Were it not for the snow that builds up around the windowsills, they would have had no water. They've had no food for five days."

"That's their choice." Wessells was heartless.

Chase continued. "How much choice do the children have, sir?"

"They're Indians. How can I explain it? I want no chances taken. Have another platoon at the ready."

Chase responded respectfully. "Yes, sir."

Wessells walked back to headquarters. Biglasky turned to Chase but before he could open his mouth, Chase spoke. "Don't say anything, Sergeant. Report to Lieutenant Simpson in the guardhouse and relay Captain Wessells' orders."

"Yes, sir."

As Biglasky walked off, Chase moved nearer a window and listened to the steady chant. What did it mean? It had a haunting beauty. A coyote howled from nearby, distracting Chase. He looked in the direction of the coyote but saw nothing but the night. In the crisp clearness, the moon cast long shadows over the snow-covered compound. The lieutenant found this situation to be an impossible test of command. He knew his men, Biglasky for certain, found the treatment of the Cheyenne to be horrible. It took every ounce of restraint he could muster to not break open the doors to those barracks and give the starving Indians food and then their freedom. But, of course, this was craziness on his part. How could he possibly understand what the commanders in Washington were faced with across all the Indian Territory.

Grandmother had said that during the time of starvation, some of the young men went crazy. "I remember Little Hump gotup and said to us, 'I want to jump out now and be killed.'"

She was sitting in bed, Ted at her side. Her breathing was labored. She grabbed Ted's arm. "Little Finger Nail and Bull Hump grabbed Little Hump and held him back until his mind came back."

After a moment, she let go of Ted.

"I seen men go nuts when we were pinned down in Korea. I understand."

"Surviving was everything for us, just like for you in battle. We were in a battle of wills. My father was determined to change our lives. Short One died under the weight of a horse. Then, in our last hours of starvation, my father told us that we might die at Fort Robinson. He said no courage is greater than that of the Cheyenne, and he insisted that we would be remembered because of it. After all, for what purpose are we here if we are not to be remembered?"

Ted understood, now more than ever.

Grandmother went on. "My sister was thirteen. She carried me that night." She looked at him with great intensity.

Ted asked, "Are you okay?"

She continued with the story. "At each of the windows, we had piled everything: our possessions, the bedding, anything to create a ramp for a quick exit out the windows. The Nail and other men loosened the pins that held the windows down. The women gathered the children near the windows." These images carried Ted once again into the world of her story.

Broken Foot Woman took Holding Woman, Ted's then five-year-old grandmother, by the hand, giving her a brave look of confidence. Pawnee Woman was helping the older women ready themselves for the escape. She moved the old ones near her daughters. As she did, Bull Hump and Little Hump had finished loosening the window pins. Bull Hump

picked up a rifle, Little Hump a club, and then they turned
to Morning Star for a signal. The others were close to ready
as Morning Star looked out over his people. He knew some
would certainly die in this flight to freedom.

The moon, now overhead, was lighting the compound as
if it were day. The sound of a window pin broke the silence.
Biglasky turned to Janzohn and asked, "Did you hear that?"
"Yeah."
"Something's up. I know it." Certain of this, Biglasky
turned to another sentry, Private Purdy, a few feet away.
"Purdy. Get over here."
Purdy walked over, patting his arms to warm them.
Biglasky gave the private an order. "Purdy, stand in here
for Janzohn, and look alive, soldier." He turned to Janzohn.
"Report to the guardhouse on the double. Tell the officer on
duty that I think the Indians are getting ready to break out."
Janzohn took off. Biglasky moved to the corner and took
in a view of the side of the barracks. He could see the sentries posted at the other end of the building, some fifty feet
away. They were distracted by the freezing weather and this
concerned the sergeant.
"Purdy, go down there and remind the other sentries
they're on duty. I don't care how cold it is."
"Yes, Sergeant," the affable private responded. He walked
off towards the far end of the barracks. He was midway
down the building when the windows of the barracks were
flung open. And in that same instant, as Purdy turned
towards the sound, a shot rang out from the middle window.

Purdy was hit and killed instantly. The Nail leapt from the window and grabbed Purdy's weapon, quickly disappearing into the shadows.

Return fire began cutting down some of the fleeing Cheyenne. The Indians' few firearms wounded a few sentries. But many of the Cheyenne escaped into the shadows around the corner of the barracks.

Within a few seconds, armed and well-prepared soldiers were filing out of the guardhouse, following Janzohn. They began shooting at the escaping Cheyenne. Lieutenant Chase ran into a position next to Janzohn, who was taking aim with his rifle.

In desperation, Chase asked, "What happened?"

"I didn't see it start, sir," Janzohn replied, firing and hitting one of the Cheyenne.

The exodus from the barracks continued as Morning Star helped Pawnee Woman, the older ones, and then his daughters out one of the windows. Ducking from the onslaught of rifle shots, he pulled them close.

Morning Star was as stern as he could be. "Don't look back. You run for the creek. No matter what happens, don't stop! I will find you."

The girls understood and began running for the shadows. Chase saw Morning Star just before he disappeared into the shadows. Broken Foot Woman, running behind her father, lost her hand grip with her younger sister. Chase watched as she turned and saw that her sister had fallen. Morning Star did not see this. Shots rang out from everywhere, and the downed girl was too frightened to move.

Broken Foot Woman ran back to her sister and Chase attempted to advance towards the two girls, trying to avoid all the cross fire. Broken Foot Woman got to Holding Woman and helped the little one climb on her back. Just as she began to carry the girl away, Broken Foot Woman was hit with a bullet to the head and fell.

The little one, seeing her sister's blood on the snow, began to cry. Broken Foot Woman rose up and grabbed her sister. She had to scream to overcome the sound of the gunfire and all the commotion. "Follow them! You know which way they went! GO!"

Holding Woman reluctantly obeyed her sister and ran off into the shadows. In that same moment, Chase came up to Broken Foot Woman and knelt in front of her, purposefully shielding her from the rifle shots.

Grandmother talked about how she ran for the creek, tears streaming down her face. Much later, her sister had told her that laying in the snow she knew she would die. Then suddenly she looked up and the soldier with the candy was there. She said it was like he was protected by the power of the *Arrows and the Hat*. Bullets did not hurt him. Broken Foot Woman looked up at Chase, his eyes were gentle in contrast to the violence surrounding them. He lifted her to his chest and stood.

Chase calmly said, "No one will hurt you." He carried Grandmother's sister away from the fight to the safety of the infirmary.

Grandmother had often said, "To my sister's dying day, she never forgot the kindness of that soldier. He saved her life."

As Chase carried Broken Foot Woman, he passed Wessells, who seemed oblivious to the lieutenant carrying one of the wounded Cheyenne. Wessells stood in shock, looking over the scene; the barracks windows broken out and his captives fleeing.

He spoke to himself. "I've failed my command. This can't happen. I will not allow them to escape, to ruin me." Then he turned to his men and yelled, "After them. Stop them!"

Wessells ran off, following the last of the escapees.

Gunshots rang out in the distance as the Cheyenne broke from the shadows and ran onto the frozen creek, falling on their hands and knees. They used their fists, clubs, butts of their rifles, anything they could to break through the ice layer so they might drink the precious water they had been deprived of for days. Rifle shots struck many of the thirst-crazed Cheyenne. A few managed to move up the river bottom towards the distant cliffs.

Holding Woman, who was still sobbing and frightened beyond comprehension, was grabbed from the shadows by Little Hump and brought to her father, Pawnee Woman, and Bull Hump.

Morning Star was relieved to see her but immediately asked, "My daughter, where is your sister?"

Crying, she pointed back to the barracks. Morning Star started to move in that direction but his sons stopped him. The advancing soldiers were everywhere.

Pawnee Woman reasoned with him. "They will kill you."

Little Hump added, "You continue. I'll keep you safe."

Bull Hump tossed Little Hump his pistol. Morning Star looked at his son in what was a moment of respect for his courage, then turned and disappeared into the night with Pawnee Woman, his little daughter, and Bull Hump.

The night was long with gunfire and death. Wessells led a charge of soldiers towards the creek. They fired at will, killing many of the escaping Cheyenne. At one point, Wessells, saber drawn, came upon an older Cheyenne man carrying a child. The man was only seeking safety but without the slightest reticence, Wessells cut the old man down with a single blow from his saber.

The soldiers advancing behind their captain rushed in the direction of Little Hump. With one round of ammunition left in his pistol, Bull Hump protected his fleeing father, mother, brother, and sister. A group of soldiers were almost upon him when Bull Hump sprang out, killing the first soldier with the blade of his knife, then another with the final shot from his pistol, before he was brought down by rifle fire.

Other soldiers discovered a group of six women and two boys, guarded by The Nail, Old Bear, and another brave. Singing Cloud and the others were huddled together, too weak to continue on. The three braves jumped out to fight. One by one, the brave, then Old Bear, and finally The Nail, were killed by the overwhelming force of soldiers.

Seeing this, Singing Cloud rose up, singing her death song, a dead child in her arms. She had no earthly purpose for continuing her life. Wessells unknowingly gifted this beautiful Cheyenne woman with her desire when he heartlessly fired from his revolver, killing Singing Cloud at close range. Then the soldiers opened fire on the other women, killing them all. Chase, with other soldiers, advanced on the scene of this carnage. They stopped in shock at Singing Cloud, fallen across The Nail. Some dropped to their knees, their guts wrenching.

Chase turned to Wessells. "Madness. Complete madness."

Wessells was in such a frenzied state he did not comprehend the words. He ran off, pursuing any Indian he could find.

Grandmother had given Ted a report of the casualties. "There were one-hundred-forty-nine of us in captivity at Fort Robinson. That winter night and for the next thirteen days, the Blue Coats pursued our people. Sixty-four Cheyenne were killed, another twenty-three wounded. Of those wounded, sixteen were women or girls."

Wessells, a madman who had tasted blood, was followed by several soldiers throughout the night. He continued pursuing the Cheyenne along the river's edge. Chase, on the other hand, was followed by some of the soldiers. He turned back and began recovering wounded Cheyenne.

Grandmother would explain. "Morning Star managed to escape with me, Pawnee Woman, and Bull Hump. He led us into the Pine Ridge Agency three weeks later. In the years since the massacre at Sand Creek, the seed of our people had scattered with the wind. With Little Wolf's people, the Cheyenne were now only a few."

Days following the breakout, the sun rose to a parade of lifeless, disheartened soldiers as they brought a wagon of wounded Cheyenne to the infirmary. The soldiers carried moaning, bleeding bodies through the door.

The post surgeon, First Lieutenant Edward Moseley, his pants hanging loosely from his suspenders, his undershirt stained in blood, continued the ordeal of repairing the bodies of so many drawn and twisted Cheyenne.

Lieutenant Chase stood in the corner, still reeling from shock. He held a folded newspaper in his hand as he looked across the room.

Moseley asked, "Will it never end?"

Chase was numb. "There aren't many left."

Moseley picked up a whiskey bottle and offered it to Chase.

The lieutenant replied, "That won't help."

"Maybe not for you." Moseley took a hit from the bottle.

Then he continued, "You shoot 'em. I'm the one expected to put them back together. And for what, so some lunatic Captain can starve them again?"

Wessells had entered and heard all of these words. With some sense of sarcasm, he responded, "It'll do no good to drink, Moseley."

Moseley turned. "Our brilliant commander." He raised the bottle as if to toast him and then a sickening sort of laugh came out. "Damn you to hell, Wessells!"

Wessells was surprisingly reserved. "You're drunk, Lieutenant."

Words were only a part of the bile Moseley felt building within his body as he responded. "And you're a filthy, sick bastard, you disgraceful little prick."

Wessells turned to Chase, ignoring Moseley. "Lieutenant Chase, I need you out here. We've got more to do."

Chase stared at his commander with contempt.

Wessells dismissed the look. "In six months, or perhaps in six weeks, this will all be forgotten."

As Wessells exited, Chase replied, "I think not."

Then, as required, he followed Wessells out of the infirmary, dropping the newspaper next to Moseley as he passed. It was the *New York Tribune*. Under the headline, the story read: *Fort Robinson Massacre. Intense indignation is manifested throughout the whole country, even among the advocates of extermination, over the barbarous treatment of the Cheyenne prisoners at Camp Robinson, previous to the recent outbreak and slaughter.*

Grandmother was disquieted as she spoke with Ted. "The captain was wrong. He knew nothing of what many people thought of our treatment. This horrible night was not forgotten."

Indeed, newspapers across the country reported stories of the inhuman conditions prior to the breakout. The government was grossly embarrassed while many influential people were outraged. Finally, Washington relented. The Cheyenne were allowed to stay with the Sioux at Pine Ridge. Some years passed and the Cheyenne were granted the land that is now Lame Deer, Montana. Morning Star had won a home for his people.

Ted moved closer to his grandmother and touched her hand. "It will never be forgotten. I promise you that. Now, you should rest, Grandma."

"I know. The time has come for the girls to say goodnight to me."

Ted picked up a medicine bottle and looked at the label. "You're supposed to take this now."

Grandmother nodded. "You go, get me some water."

Ted started to get up but she reached out and stopped him. "You tell this story. They will want to know." She spoke those familiar words with such finality, it was as if he had never heard them.

Ted sensed the difference in tone but quickly shrugged it off with a smile of assurance. "Of course I will. You know that."

She added, "Think of the future, Ted, my son. Don't live with what is the past."

He leaned down close to her, looked at her wonderfully wise face for a moment, then kissed her.

"Now go, I am thirsty."

"I'll be right back with the water."

After he left, she leaned her head back on the pillow. A moment passed and then it seemed to her that someone had entered. She strained to see. "Ted, is that you?" But there was only silence. Then her face relaxed and she spoke again. "I understand. There are two roads. The white man's road and the Indian's road. Neither knows the road of the other. Ever has it been, and still it is today." After a few moments, she closed her eyes. Her breathing was heavy and then suddenly it stopped.

CHAPTER 15
CARLISLE

Mourners were gathered for the traditional Cheyenne wake at the Mennonite church hall. They included the family, Imogene, and some fifty others. Men, women, and children had come to celebrate grandmother Holding Woman's life. Pictures of her were mounted on a bulletin board, which rested on an easel. Alongside were some of grandmother's possessions, including her rifle. Across the room a buffet style spread of food was being set up by church helpers.

Ruthie was standing with Ted next to the pictures of her great grandma. She had prepared as best she could for this moment when she would address the gathering in honor of her great grandmother. Her dad's hand felt warm as she held it. She was trying very hard to keep from crying. It was a difficult task but, like the grownup she saw herself as, she believed she had the strength to do this. After all, she was the older sister, the one who had picked her mother off the floor on many a night, the one who had taken care of her sister before they moved in with Grandpa Oliver and Grandma Elizabeth. Like her great grandmother, she had learned very young to take care of her family.

Ruthie looked up at her dad. He gave her a nod that said it was time to begin. The room quieted, Ruthie unfolded the paper on which she had copied a poem she thought perfect for this day, and then she began.

In the universe so vast
Our love can only intensify.
Though I am still an outcast
And on you I rely.
We all start with innocence
Then love brings a haze
Which seems to condense
And leave us in a daze.

Ruthie folded the paper. She looked out, into the room. "We all miss you, Grandma. You brought us lots of love and you made us feel welcome. You understood everything. And you taught me so much. I love you, Grandma." Then she looked up at her dad.

He gave her a reassuring look and said, "That was beautiful, Ruthie."

Ruthie crossed in front of many friends of Holding Woman as she moved to join Oliver and Elizabeth, who were sitting with Myra and Imogene. Ted stayed by the photos of his grandmother.

After a moment, Ted picked up grandma's rifle. "Holding Woman had this for a long time. She was really proud of it and used it well." He stepped over to an older woman, Thelma. "Thelma, you knew Grandma since she came home from Carlisle. She would want you to have this."

Thelma took the rifle and looked it over. She raised it up, sighting in on a spot across the room. Then she said, "Thanks, Ted. I'll damn sure use it next season."

Ted smiled. "Looks like you will."

Ted moved to the photos of Grandma. "Before we give Grandma's other things away, there's something to remember about her. What I want to say is, I've never known anyone with more courage than she had. When she was six, after surviving that trek north from Oklahoma, the relentless pursuit by the Army, the loss of Short One, then the starvation and the cold, followed by the breakout from Fort Robinson, she faced another unimaginable journey."

Ted's description that followed was new to only a few of the people who were gathered. Some had experienced firsthand what he was about to describe; others had relatives that survived it. But to many of the younger family members, this was a new story. They were about to hear the experience of the first class of Indian students taken from their families to the Carlisle School in Pennsylvania.

Ted began with the date. "It was October, 1879, just months after my grandmother, her father Morning Star, and the others had settled. The government in Washington had decided that special schools should be started that would teach the children of the many Indian tribes the same things that the white children were being taught in their schools. This was what the white people explained to Morning Star when he attempted to convince the old Chief that he should let some of the Cheyenne go to school with him.

"The headmaster for the school, Richard Henry Pratt, had come to the reservation to recruit children. He convinced parents that this was the right thing to do. The first children chosen for this were from the Cheyenne and our neighbors at Red Cloud, the Sioux."

Ted explained, "The U.S. government had given a deserted military base to Pratt, who was a former officer in the Tenth Cavalry. He recruited a former teacher and Indian interpreter, Miss Mather, to assist him. Pratt was certain that he could take Indian children away from their tribal influences and turn them into white people. Of course, he explained this purpose differently to the government than he had to our families.

"The day that Holding Woman said goodbye to Morning Star and Pawnee Woman was filled with the tears of the many children that were leaving their homes for boarding school. She and eighty other children were taken from their families and shipped by train to central Pennsylvania. Their ages ranged from six to sixteen."

Ted described the scene with such emotion that it came to life in the minds of this gathering. "Holding Woman stood in front of Morning Star. He handed her a wolf-skin pouch, placing it tenderly in her hands and folding her fingers around it.

"Morning Star tried to comfort her. 'This bundle will keep the strength of your mother and me with you. Protect it. You have to learn their way of life.'

"Holding Woman bravely responded, 'I understand, father.'

"The children were loaded into the passenger car at the rear of the train. All of them pressed against the windows to get their last look at family as the train rolled out of the station. Five long days and nights later the same train rolled into Carlisle, having traveled through a rainstorm for hours.

"Holding Woman, her face against the glass, looked on in fear. The rainfall had just stopped and many citizens were looking on at the arriving train. Some held umbrellas, others torches."

The scene continued to unfold as Ted described the arrival. "As the children disembarked, the onlookers crowded them. The children's dark eyes were wide with fright as they moved through the aggressive crowd. They were mostly wearing buckskin, some were covered with blankets, and they all had long, black braided hair.

"As Pratt and Mather led the children from the train, a reporter was getting the crowd's reactions to their arrival. The children heard comments such as, 'How do you feel about having these wild children in the community?' or 'I'm anxious to see what the savages look like.' And, 'How do you civilize the children of the people who murdered Custer?'"

Ted continued, "Those questions and answers moved with the children until they boarded the waiting wagon that would take them from the station, following the black carriage that carried Pratt and Mather to the school.

"As the carriage and wagon rolled into the deserted military base, the children peered out at their new home. It was dark and foreboding, like a ghost town. There was no lighting, nothing to suggest warmth. Being winter, the trees were barren, the grass brown.

"A man with a lantern greeted the black carriage. A dim light came from within the barracks as the children followed Pratt up the stairs and inside the dormitory. Once inside, the man lit an oil lamp hanging from the ceiling. As the light filled the room, Pratt walked to the center, stopped, and took in the sight. His look was one of disbelief. There was nothing in the room. The wood floor was clean, but there was not one stick of furniture.

"Pratt inquired. 'Where are the beds?'

"Miss Mather stepped in beside Pratt as the children stepped in behind the two of them.

"The man replied. 'They haven't arrived yet, sir. Nothing is here.'

"Pratt was shocked. 'But the Bureau of Indian Affairs . . . they promised me that the bedding, the food, the clothing . . . that it would all be here no later then last week.'

"The man could only repeat the information. 'I am sorry. Nothing has arrived.' Pratt shook his head. 'What am I to do?'

"Miss Mather offered a cold answer. 'The children will have to sleep on the floor. They are certainly used to conditions worse than this.'

"Pratt pleaded. 'You at least have blankets?'

"The man responded, almost embarrassed, 'A few.'

"Pratt quickly asked, 'Bring them, please.'"

More of the storm arrived later that first evening. Rainwater ran down the windows. Lightning cast a moment of electric blue across the room, followed by the expected crash of thunder. The children lay on the floor covered in blankets, very alone, very frightened.

Ted continued, "It was many more days until all the furniture and supplies arrived. In the days that followed, the systematic changes and elimination of their culture began." Ted painted a verbal picture of the children being lined up, waiting turns in the barber's chair. One by one, as they were processed past the scissors of the town barber, their long hair was cut off. Many of the girls wept as their precious hair fell to the floor.

Ted remembered. "In the Cheyenne custom at that time, to cut off our hair was an act of *mourning*. The loss of the children's hair was just another trauma they had to endure. Their hair was so much a part of who they were." Ted described how Holding Woman spoke of her hair being cut off.

"Tears ran down her cheeks as she saw her braids laying on the floor. Another staff member, Miss Hyde, led Holding Woman from the barber to a table from which a blue woolen blouse and skirt, along with black leather shoes were handed to her. The boy behind her received a blue military uniform and black shoes.

"Later, all the children, dressed in blue, with the stiff new shoes, filed out the door with instructions to bring their personal clothes. None of them were comfortable and not one was happy in those inflexible and confining garments. Having been accustomed to handmade garments of soft deerskin and comfortable moccasins on their feet, this would be a natural reaction. Miss Mather, accompanied by Miss Hyde, collected the children's personal clothes.

"As Grandmother joined the others, she handed her clothes to Miss Mather, who sternly grabbed the girl's precious bundle. She was reluctant to give it up. Their comfortable moccasins and loose-fitting buckskin clothes, made for them by their mothers and grandmothers, all they were allowed to bring with them from their homes, were taken in that moment. The children watched, pained by the sight, as all their possessions were placed in a heap and set on fire.

"And then there was the giving of names. The children were lined up in a classroom. The single column faced Miss Mather's desk. On the blackboard behind her were chalk-written columns of Christian names. Miss Hyde stood with a pointer as Miss Mather explained that each child would take the pointer and choose the name they wanted. After that, they would only be known by that name.

"The children did not understand all of this. They looked at this stern woman, not quite knowing what to do. Miss Hyde picked the first boy, handed him the pointer, and gestured to the board.

"'Pick one.' Hyde demanded.

"The boy looked at her, puzzled. He looked back at the others for help but they were equally baffled and wide-eyed with fear. Miss Hyde slapped her hands together getting the boy's attention. She pointed to the board again.

"'Pick one, now,' She insisted.

"The boy pointed to the board, copying her gesture. The pointer landed on the name, *Luther*.

"'Luther,' Hyde exclaimed.

"While Miss Hyde erased the name Luther, Miss Mather quickly wrote the name on a piece of white cloth and handed it to Miss Hyde. She in turn pinned the name tag on the boy.

"The renaming was just one of the many atrocities the children had to withstand. It was part of the attempt to kill the Indian in them, as was the entire Carlisle experience. Eliminating their native language was another major effort.

"It was strictly forbidden for the children to speak in their native Indian tongue. They were to only speak in English. To speak in any other language was strictly prohibited at Carlisle. This rule was enforced with a harshness not fit for a prison let alone a school for children. A military-type discipline was common, but a vicious response to certain behavior became expected at any given moment. Luther was the first to make this painful discovery. It happened on a day the children were lined up in front of their beds for the first of their military-style inspections. This would be the day of Luther's baptism in horror.

"The dormitory master was a severe looking man of forty with a pronounced esophagus. As he was making his inspection, Luther made the mistake of muttering a comment in Sioux to his friend, referring to the dormitory master as 'chicken neck.' "The dormitory master heard the Sioux words and saw that it was Luther who had uttered them. The man charged towards Luther, catching him by the shirt collar and then by the neck. The dormitory master lifted Luther off the floor as the boy struggled to breathe, his wind being choked off by the tightness of the shirt collar and the grip on his throat.

"The Master warned him. 'Don't you ever speak in Indian again. Understand me, redskin?'

"Luther was continuing to struggle. The master threw him across the room with such force that Luther suffered a broken collarbone.

"That was the night Holding Woman began sketching her memories of her family and the flight home from the south in this book." Ted held up the journal. "Somehow, she managed to hide it from the school officials. She introduced me to it just before she left us. I believe this little book helped my grandmother survive her years away at school. You must see this. It will remind you of the sacrifice that brought us here."

Ted put the journal on a table, and then continued, explaining more of the enormities of Carlisle. "Physical abuse was only part of it. Tuberculosis and smallpox, and the severe stress of being separated from family, took a horrible toll. In Carlisle's graveyard, wooden crosses marked the many gravesites. Indian bodies and bones are in museums all over this country.

"But the coldest of all these are the bones of those frightened, lonely children who had no parent to comfort them, who died from illnesses they suffered at Carlisle. Fortunately for all of us, Holding Woman returned. She had the pleasure of seeing her father settled in the Rosebud Valley, the future home of the Cheyenne."

The older people nodded in agreement, as each remembered their own experience.

Ted looked across the room and saw that the food was ready. "Now, it's time for us to eat. Thank you all for bringing food. Please, help yourselves. After we eat, let's talk more about Grandmother."

As the families moved to the food table, Oliver approached Ted, who greeted his father with a hug. "Dad. How you holding up?" He patted Oliver on the shoulder. Oliver sighed and shook his head. Ted asked, "You gonna speak?"

"There's a few words I'll say." Oliver sat down. "Sit down with me here."

Ted sat next to him.

Oliver looked at his son. "You're quite the talker. I heard about your speech at Busby the other day."

Ted looked down for a moment. "I know that wasn't good for you, Dad. Sorry."

"Don't be. You made quite an impression. Guess Grandma was right. You are the one to carry on the tradition."

"I don't know. I tell a few stories. I enjoy it."

"I think it's more than that, son. You are a storyteller. You know how to reach the folks. These people. They've all heard the story of Carlisle before, but never like this."

Ted shrugged, not ready to accept this accolade. "Well, right now I've got to find a job."

"You ought to get involved with the Tribal Council. They need young blood like yours."

"To do what?" Ted inquired.

"Help shape our future. What else?"

Ted doubted the value of this idea. "The board's filled with the old ones. They're not going to listen to me. And they're afraid of change."

"The tribe is growing. The board is going up to sixteen members. Some of you younger men need to get involved."

"I don't know, Dad."

"Son, in one afternoon you stirred up a ruckus at Busby School. You want to make a difference within our schools? Well, your opportunity is with the Tribal Council, not as a janitor. Think about it."

Oliver looked towards Grandma's picture and added the hook. "For her."

Oliver walked off to the food table. Ted looked around the room, at the people talking, the occasional laugh from a story about Holding Woman, and the general feeling of warmth. He was lost in his thoughts as Imogene sat beside him. After a moment, she reached for his hand, taking it in hers. He looked at her, then at their hands. After a moment, he placed his other hand on top of hers. Six months later they were married.

CHAPTER 16

COUNCIL OF SIXTEEN

The main intersection of the town was different. It now had two paved roads. It was May of 1972. The town had grown with the addition of a bank, a few commercial stores, and those paved streets.

Winters are long in this northern country. Some years it will snow in June. But this year the winter had passed. A 1967 Ford sedan, driven by Imogene, pulled out of the market parking lot. She stopped at the intersection, waiting on crossing traffic. A Willie Nelson tune was finishing on the radio. She changed the dial, stopping on a news broadcast where a local news commentator was giving his afternoon report. "On the national scene, there's no end in sight for the war in Vietnam. Amazing, since President Johnson promised us that none of our boys would shed blood on foreign soil. So much for campaign promises. And now President Nixon is increasing the bombing."

Imogene crossed the main road and headed down a smaller highway. She approached the Tribal Council building and made the left turn into the lot. Ted saw her and walked towards the car.

The news broadcast was continuing. "B-52s continue their daily runs on Cambodia. This while the body bags keep coming home."

Ted got to the driver's door as she parked. He immediately flirted. "Hey, lady. Doing anything later?"

"I don't know. What did you have in mind, soldier?"

Doreen Pond, mid-twenties, passed the car.

Ted nodded to her. "I'll be inside in a minute."

Doreen called out, "Hi, Imogene."

Imogene replied with a smile, "Hey, Doreen." Then she looked up at Ted. "So what time do you want me back here?"

"I don't know. Why don't you stick around and watch the Council meeting?"

"What, sit in that smoke-filled room and listen to people argue?"

"Sometimes it gets pretty exciting. People get mad, even cuss me out."

"If one of those people starts that, I'll go bop them on the head. You know I won't sit still like some dummy."

This made Ted laugh. Then he thought about her first question. "I'll get a ride home. See you when I get there."

Imogene remembered something. "Charlie's son is home from Vietnam. Maybe you could talk to him? I heard he's drinking."

Ted had a strong reaction. "No wonder. Six months in the jungle in a kill or be killed situation. Then they fly them home. How are they supposed to cope?" Neither one of them had an answer. After a moment, he walked off.

The years that passed since Holding Woman's death had seen the natural progression of time. Both Ruthie and Myra had finished their schooling, married, and started their own families. During those years, Ted had worked hard for the Cheyenne Nation. He was now a member of the Tribal Council, the voting body that had the authority to govern the business of the Cheyenne.

He had fought many fights on behalf of his people, not the least of which was with the corporate interests that ran coal mining operations on reservation land. Seven coal mining companies, as major as Coneco Corporation, had negotiated leases through the Bureau of Indian Affairs that granted the companies mineral rights to certain Cheyenne lands. The intent of these companies was to strip mine the rich coal deposits found in that region.

These leases could have been a road map to an ecological rape of the landscape in Lame Deer, wherein millions of dollars in mineral resources would have been the justification. When the Cheyenne, led by a group that Ted organized, challenged these leases with the BIA, they were told the Cheyenne had no say in the matter and were therefore refused any interaction with officials of these coal mining companies or with the BIA.

Ted marshaled the Cheyenne effort to stop those leases from being developed. The legal effort was carried all the way to the Supreme Court where an almost immediate verdict was rendered in which all leases were canceled. As important, the Bureau of Indian Affairs was found to have committed thirty-seven counts of fraud at the expense of the

Cheyenne Nation. In addition, the companies involved were ordered by the Supreme Court to pay reparations to the Cheyenne.

To put it simply, Ted was not afraid of anyone or any company. Whether a land lease was being violated, water rights being misused, logging rights misrepresented, it did not matter. Ted was a fighter and had long since decided to be vocal on behalf of his tribe. But this quality of his, to be outspoken, was not to be confused with an arrogance or belligerent attitude so common during the post-Vietnam period. Ted had learned how to go with the flow of life, dodge the bullets, and pick his battles wisely. He charmed his way through what could have been many hostile conflicts.

Arguments with other board members were common, too. Ted had first been hampered by the elders on the board who were afraid of change. These people had been deprived for so long that the fear of losing what little they had most times outweighed what they might gain from another conflict with the government. Ted's voice was fresh and seemingly unconcerned about such timidity. In reality, he had many sleepless nights worrying about what might be given up in one area to gain in another. As time progressed and more young minds joined the Council, the essential attitude became more progressive.

One area of the Council's business that remained very unsettled for Ted was education. The circumstance of the BIA-run schools was not much different then he had experienced as a student. Gone were the "Carlisle" boarding schools. Now what existed across all the Indian Nations were schools that met quotas and processed numbers of students without any concern as to the quality of their education. Ted demanded accountability. He wanted tribal involvement in curriculum. Ted mostly wanted parents to be allowed onto school boards so that they would be participating in their own children's education.

That night in May of 1972 the *Tribal Council of Sixteen* Cheyenne was meeting at a long table in the Council chamber. Those members present included Ted; Llevando "Cowboy" Fisher, mid-twenties; and Doreen, who sat across from Ted. They were studying a letter of proposal. Alan Rowland, the Council president, in his late-sixties, was seated in the center. Thomas Shoulder Blade, who was in his mid-sixties, was at Rowland's side. They were flanked by Raymond Spane and Dennis Limber Hand. The balance of the members ranged in age from late twenties to fifty. Behind the Council table stood the American flag and the Morning Star flag.

Seated directly in front of Rowland was the BIA Superintendent, James Tucker. At his side was Joe Coyote, a Lakota/Cheyenne. The two were flanked by four men, three Indians and one white. All six were dressed in suits, a stark contrast to the rest of the room.

The room was crowded with tribal members. This was a standing room only meeting. There was much disagreement and arguing taking place. Kenneth Wolf Trap, early thirties and dressed in his military fatigues, a '70s radical, tried to address the room. Rowland pounded the gavel and settled the room down.

Rowland called out. "Quiet! Let Kenneth finish."

The room settled.

Kenneth was a little awkward at the microphone. "I fought in Nam. Almost died there. I come home and these government people tell me the BIA may close our only school. And my kids are going to be bused all the way to Harden? Well I say, bullshit! I am an Indian. They're not going to do that to my kids."

"Yeahs" of agreement filled the crowd.

Inspired by the reaction, he continued. "We can't let the government close our school!"

The crowd liked this and gave their support. While these shouts of agreement came from the floor, Ted got up and moved to the center to face Tucker. Ted had the proposal letter in his hand. Rowland pounded the gavel. The crowd slowly quieted.

Ted took the microphone. "Tucker, here's what I think of the BIA proposal." Ted tore the proposal in half. The room loved this and roared more approval.

Tucker was a very officious type. He clearly did not like this kind of crowd, finding them to be unruly.

Looking around at the excitement, he commented, "That'll get us nowhere."

Ted calmed the crowd and then turned to Kenneth. "Tell me, Kenneth, did you go to BIA school?"

"You know I did. Just like you, at Busby."

Ted teased Kenneth and the crowd with his question in response. "And you want to keep it open?"

A little laughter followed.

"Well, it's the only school we got."

Ted agreed. "That's true. So, something's better than nothing. Is that it?"

Kenneth thought about that.

A voice from the crowd called out. "What else can we do?"

Ted seized on the question. "We should petition the BIA to give us the contract to run our own school. We'll manage the operation ourselves."

A lot of rumbling followed that comment.

Tucker found that thought ludicrous. "That's impossible. It's never been done. The Bureau of Indian Affairs has always controlled Indian education."

Joe Coyote spoke up. Perhaps Tucker thought the voice of an Indian, even though on the government's side, would be useful in the moment. "It's too dangerous. You could lose the whole thing."

Ted quickly turned that around. "What are you worried about? We've been losing our kids to substandard education for years."

A few noises of agreement filled the room.

Ted added emphasis. "They graduate from BIA schools and can't pass entrance exams for state run community colleges. What choices are they left with? What opportunity awaits our kids after they graduate from Busby?" Ted looked right at Tucker. "Do you think our seventy percent unemployment rate sounds inspiring?"

Crowd agreements were voiced. Ted picked up the emotion and played to the room. "When parents, like me and you, try to speak to the BIA school superintendent about the curriculum, or the quality of the teachers, the door is closed in our face."

More crowd noises of agreement filled the room. It was beginning to overwhelm Tucker.

Ted faced Tucker and challenged him. "We are not welcome on the school board. Why?"

Tucker warned him and the crowd. "Don't try to go against the government!"

Ted turned to the rest of the Council members. "We can hire a lawyer. I think we should file a petition. It's our right."

More crowd approval was swelling.

Tucker had nowhere to go in this dialog. "You want to waste tribal money?"

Ted snapped back. "We're talking about our kids. There's nothing better to spend money on, as I see things. We want to have a voice in what and how our children are taught."

The crowd was almost out of control. It took Ted a full minute to quiet them. This was now a lot more than a meeting. Ted realized as he was speaking these thoughts, a real idea was forming.

Ted approached Tucker again and, with a very sincere tone, pleaded, "Look, we don't want to teach our kids to hate the government. We want them to respect Washington and what it is supposed to stand for. But how can they learn to respect the government, if we don't?"

Tucker conferred with Coyote, shaking his head. Coyote got up and addressed the room. "This sort of thing could upset everything. The BIA won't like this. You're risking everything for some crazy idea."

Ted was truly disappointed in such a reply. "If we don't do something now, our kids will continue to be second-class citizens. And so will their kids, and this will go on and on." Murmurs began building from the crowd.

Cowboy Fisher rose and called out, "I want to put forth a motion that we take a Council vote on the matter of hiring a lawyer to advise the Northern Cheyenne Tribal Council on the legalities of a petition for the first tribal run school."

Doreen stood. "I second the motion."

Cowboy and Doreen both looked over to Rowland who conferred with his colleagues for a moment, then turned to the room. "We'll take a vote with a show of hands. Those in favor of the motion to hire a lawyer to review the matter of a petition filing with the BIA for a contract to operate the school at Busby, raise your hands."

Ted, Doreen, Cowboy, Rowland, and ten other board members raised their hands. That being a majority, the crowd erupted with cheers of approval.

The crowded meeting had finally ended. Mostly happy people were filing out of the building. Ted, Doreen, and Cowboy stepped into the parking lot together.

Cowboy asked Ted a question with a slight twinge of sarcasm. "Well, okay. We got ourselves a fight. What's next?"

Ted was quick with his answer. "Cowboy, we need the right lawyer. We need someone who likes to fight."

As the three thought about that truism, Doreen quietly spoke. "Ted, I've got an idea."

Before he could inquire, an older man from the meeting passed the three of them. He stopped and looked right at

Ted. The tone of this elder was to scold Ted for such a brash idea. "This plan of yours? Not smart. What gives you the idea you can beat the government? You think you're wiser than the rest of us who have been fighting with the BIA for years? You might make everything worse. We might lose the school completely. Then what would you say to us?"

The old man walked off, leaving Ted struck by his words. After several silent moments, Ted responded to his comrades. "What if he's right?"

Ted carried that question home with him. It plagued him most of the night. Imogene was well versed and experienced in Ted's private insecurities. He would never let anyone know how often he doubted himself, except her. But even as his wife, she only knew some of his fears.

For Ted, it was not to question his methods or his intent. It was always a question of what was really possible. He went on for several hours with Imogene, asking, "Who do I think I'm fooling? The BIA will never listen. All the lawyers we could hire will never make those slick Washington politicians listen to us."

After he'd smoked a dozen cigarettes and drank a pot of coffee and talked for two hours straight, he finally stopped.Imogene, with her quiet and direct way, reminded Ted that the truth was in the question, probably the same question that Morning Star had asked himself many times. "What is there to lose that has not already been lost?"

It took Imogene about two minutes to turn Ted back in the right direction. As she spoke, she brought his thoughts to where they had started. "In this moment, as it was a hundred years earlier and will be a hundred years from now, it is all about the future, and that means it is about the children."

Ted just looked at her in silence. Imogene went back to her beading. She had said what needed to be said. After a couple of minutes, Ted got up and took her in his arms. "That's what I love about you. You keep it simple. You keep me on the ground. You remind me not to get lost in all my thoughts."

They embraced for a moment and then kissed.

CHAPTER 17
GROUNDWORK

Doreen opened her front door to Ted. It was a modest home. A small living room opening to a kitchen-dining area and two bedrooms with one bath. Doreen's husband, Leland, who was twenty-eight, sat at a desk-size table in the front room. He was a formidable looking man with a kind face. Leland sat behind stacks of legal books and several piles of papers that were in process. A pair of folding chairs faced the table. Leland was finishing a phone call as Ted and Doreen approached him. He was wired on cigarettes and coffee.

Leland was signing off. "Okay. I'll see you at the courthouse. Right."

Leland hung up. His demeanor turned friendly immediately. "Hi."

Doreen gestured to Ted. "Leland, this is Ted."

Leland stood, reached across the table to shake hands with the stranger. "Ted. Heard lots about you from the wife. Have a seat."

As they sat down, Ted turned on the charm. "Busy new practice, huh?"

Leland gestured to the phone. "That's a water rights issue. Since I set up shop, seems all my time is spent fighting the

BIA." Ted laughed. "With them around, you'll never run out of work."

Leland got to the point. "So, you want to petition for a contract to run the first ever Indian reservation school."

Ted responded. "That's pretty much it."

Leland raised his eyebrows. "Well, I hope you like to fight. You couldn't have picked a tougher battle."

Doreen piped in. "Why should anything BIA be easy?"

Leland shifted into his legal banter. "Research, the precedents, filings, the court time, it'll suck more out of you than the dry August wind."

Ted commented. "We know there are expenses."

"That's the easy part." Leland leaned forward. "What teaching experience do any of you have?"

Before Ted could answer, Leland continued. "What do any of you know about academic curriculum? Grading curves? SAT test preparation? Federal minimum standards?"

Ted was a little surprised and defensive. "We're parents with real concerns."

Leland countered, "As if that matters. Look, the BIA hires professionals. They're trained teachers with credentials."

Ted chuckled. "Most of them couldn't get a teaching job anywhere else."

"But the personnel files have their credentials that say those people are certified. Do you actually think the bozos in D.C. are going to turn this over to you because of your . . . 'real concerns'?"

Ted's eyebrows furrowed. "Whose side are you on?"

Leland grinned. "Yours. Look, I know our schools are the worst, and I understand what you're feeling. But

Washington? No way. They're into budgets, allocations, and with something like this, the path of least resistance. You! You want to rock their boat."

Ted agreed. "Yeah. Before it sinks with our kids and future on board."

Leland thought on it for a moment. "What's our strategy?"

Ted was surprised by the question. "That's your job, isn't it?"

Leland shook his head, then laughed. As he spoke, he made notes. "Tucker's the classic bureaucrat. So, we'll drown him in paper. Doreen, our friends at UCLA can help. We're going to need statistics from the department of education on the national standards and levels of achievement across the fifty states." He ripped off a piece of note paper and handed it to her. "Call Harry on campus. There's his number."

Doreen took the paper and started making notes as well. Ted realized that Leland was the man for the job.

Leland continued with his line of thought. "We've got to find someone who can get into the BIA, Department of the Interior, for statistics on Indian education."

Later that evening Ted and Imogene sat at the kitchen table drinking coffee, having their after dinner smoke.

Ted was winding through the conversation he had with Leland and Doreen. "They've both got friends at UCLA from their graduate school days. Doreen said I'd be surprised how much help she'll pull in from student activists."

Imogene was almost indifferent. "Well, good. You're all set."

"Not quite. We've got to get inside the BIA to find out about reservation schools." He was looking at her with an unusually intense attitude.

Imogene wondered why the intensity seemed directed at her? He was not looking for reassurance. But she was curious. "How you gonna do that, get inside the BIA?"

He was quick to ask, "I was hoping you might help."

Imogene took a last drag and stamped the cigarette out, grabbed her coffee cup and stepped over to the sink. He followed her.

As he got to the sink, she turned to him. "What if that old man from last night was right? Have you thought about what happens when you start pushing the buttons at the BIA and they close Busby down? Then what?"

Ted backed up. He had not expected her to throw the old man's words back to him. They had been through all that last night. She was the one who reassured him. Now she was questioning the very thing she convinced him of.

Ted found his resolve. "What happened to all those things you reminded me of last night? I can't live that way, being afraid to take a chance."

She replied with a certain tenderness. "I've thought about this all day. I'm really not sure what to think. Ted, you're taking a chance with the kids' education. Leland was right to ask you what you really know about teaching."

He began to tighten up. This conflict suddenly seemed unfair.

She continued. "I know the Indian teaching tradition of grandmothers works for us here. But how are you going to get anyone else to understand that, when the white man's government doesn't understand anything else about our people? And they have shown no interest in learning about us, either."

He poured another cup of coffee and lit a cigarette as Imogene went on flushing out her concerns. "I mean, we've got a hundred years of experience with the government not listening, and breaking the treaties and the promises. Sure, you tell great stories and it sounds real good in the Tribal Council with everyone whooping it up. Well, that ain't the BIA office, and it sure as hell isn't Washington."

He was now glaring at her. "You finished?" he asked.

She shrugged.

Ted went the direct route. "Will you help me, us?"

A long moment passed as she considered.

Ted added, "You've got access to the superintendent's files. That's what we need."

Imogene poured another cup of coffee and walked back to the table. She took a seat and with great deliberation added two spoonfuls of sugar to her coffee. She stirred four times. Ted was counting. Then, with a conciliatory tone, she asked him, "What do you want me to do? How do I help you?"

CHAPTER 18

HIGH HEEL
SNOW BOOTS

The Bureau of Indian Affairs building was modern dark
brick with lots of windows. The parking lot was slushy from
six inches of fresh but quickly melting snow. This structure
stood apart from everything in Lame Deer. It was an edifice
with no soul, erected on soil that once was grazing land for
the buffalo. Placing a teepee in the heart of Manhattan
would be just as incongruous. The difference here, however,
was that the government has an amazing way, in some
instances, of spending money on programs that really do
nothing for the problem they are supposed to serve.

Ted's Ford sedan was waiting to turn left from the highway into the BIA parking lot. He watched traffic as Leland,
wired on coffee, rifled through legal papers on his lap. He
leaned into the backseat and looked through one of two file
boxes. While this was happening, Ted noticed a woman in
the BIA parking lot struggling to walk in the snow. She was
a sight to behold, but not because Ted enjoyed people's
struggles. Rather, this was a case of someone being dressed
in all the wrong clothing for the moment.

Ted began to laugh. "You've got to see this."

Leland looked up to see a thirty-five-year-old black woman, Dorothy Deville, walking from a rented Buick to the building. Wearing high heel shoes, a fur jacket, and carrying a briefcase, she was trying to get herself across the parking lot without ruining her shoes. She was not pleased.

Ted looked at Dorothy in disbelief.

Leland commented as he went back to his paper brigade. "Big city folks."

The traffic cleared and Ted pulled into the lot, parking in a just opened spot near the building entrance. Dorothy struggled past their car as Ted and Leland were getting out.

Ted called to Dorothy, "Storm caught you, huh?"

Dorothy was none too friendly. "You'd think they could clean this snow off the sidewalks. It was bad enough at the airport, what with no porters and all."

Ted laughed to himself. "You're in the country, ma'am.

Sorry you couldn't find a porter."

She had no comment as she continued. Ted gave Leland a raised eyebrow as he grabbed one of the file boxes. As he passed Dorothy, he tipped his hat, adding in a friendly tone, "Hope you have a good day."

Ted and Leland were meeting with James Tucker. A U.S. flag stood on a pole in the corner of his office. It had an official picture of President Richard Nixon. The men sat at a conference table. The file boxes they had carried in sat at the other end.

Tucker was looking over the petition as Leland talked him through it.

Leland's final comment summed the whole thing up. "It all boils down to local authority over the school."

Tucker was annoyed. "I can read, Mr. Pond." Tucker put down the paper. "You know, Mr. Rising Sun, you have to accept that flag."

Tucker had gestured to the U.S. flag in the corner. Ted looked at it. After a moment, he responded, "Accept the flag! You mean like joining the army and fighting in two wars for my country? That kind of accepting the flag?"

Tucker was almost sarcastic. "I'm not asking for your service record. The flag still flies on the reservation, even though it is Cheyenne land. The Bureau has responsibility for the schools, that's the way it has always been."

Tucker slid the petition back to Leland.

Leland picked up the conversation, trying to get back into some kind of positive dialog. "Busby's students don't meet educational standards. You're just processing them. You have teachers over there that don't care. The records and statistics are in the boxes."

Tucker was defensive. "It's not easy getting qualified people to come here. And you actually think you can do better?"

Ted jumped in. "That's right."

Dorothy entered as Leland pushed the paper back to Tucker.

Leland added, "We're filing that tomorrow. Might want to keep it, so you can get a jump start on your answer."

Dorothy walked over to Tucker's side. "Jim. What's this about?" She picked up the petition.

Tucker turned in his chair to respond to her. "Ah, these two men are from the Cheyenne Tribal Council. Ted Rising

Sun and Leland Pond, their attorney. Gentlemen, this is Miss Dorothy Deville. She oversees education for the Bureau. She's in from D.C. They think Indians can run the school better than the Bureau."

Dorothy arrogantly flipped through the petition. She looked over at Ted as she put the petition down. "I flew in here today to discuss budgets. The Bureau's been having some serious discussion about cutting the appropriation for the Busby School. They asked me to make some recommendations. You file that—Indian petition, well let me just say that's not going to help keep the school open."

Ted took a moment before responding. "Miss Deville, we have a people problem here. Things being labeled Indian, or white, or black. This is about our kids and what's the best thing for them. Color doesn't matter."

She hit him with a response of someone who was so caught up with the aesthetic, the appearance of efficiency, that they could not see, nor had they even bothered to look at, the substance of the issue.

She simply said, "Quotas do matter."

Ted would not accept that. "Whether I'm half Cheyenne or a third Sioux shouldn't be a criteria. What a school board needs to look at is the appropriateness of the material being taught."

Dorothy was just staring blankly, giving off no emotion. Ted was becoming more passionate. "When my children came home from school, I used to ask myself: What are they going to be? What do they learn about life's values in school?"

Dorothy responded, "Learning to read and write, to do basic math and basic history, that's the curriculum we have."

Ted countered, "But are academics alone the reliable and true foundation to prepare them?"

"Maybe the students aren't capable of more." She delivered those words with ice.

This coldness, however, did not deter Ted. "Let parents participate with the school. The elders have so much wisdom to offer. It comes from life experience, not from outdated textbooks."

She looked at the petition again. "If you want to argue this, come to Washington. Mr. Tucker will arrange a meeting." Ted was not willing to give up. "Miss Deville, Mr. Tucker, we are not trying to attack you. The children are the issue. Your department is given a budget each year. Why not do the very best you can with the money you have to spend? Why not let us help? If we work on this together, we can improve the situation."

Dorothy made no comment but, "We've got pressing business now."

Ted got up, leaned toward her, and pressed his finger on the table. "When would like to meet in Washington?"

Dorothy remained silent, her jaws tight. Leland was watching how cool Ted was. "Next month, at the earliest. I'll have to check the director's calendar."

Ted politely replied, "Please do that. I can be there within twenty-four-hours' notice."

Dorothy finished the meeting with, "Tucker will contact you."

Ted added, "By the way, Miss Deville. We welcome the snow. It brings us our water."

Dorothy's jaw tightened with that comment. Ted and Leland walked out of the office.

As Ted and Leland crossed the parking lot Ted gazed off towards the horizon. Leland was wondering if the attitude in the office would change the fire in Ted's belly. "Bureaucratic lip service. What's right means nothing."

Ted continued his gaze. "Imagine a hundred years ago, to see this land taken over and controlled by people like that."

After a moment, Ted stepped to the car.

Doreen and Imogene pulled up next to them. They got out and rushed to Ted and Leland, who were surprised by their arrival.

Imogene asked, "Did you already have the meeting?"

Ted shrugged. "We just finished. Why?"

Doreen handed Leland a telegram. He began reading it.

Imogene pointed to the telegram. "Look at what Doreen has. You won't believe what it says."

"The United States Senate!" Leland read aloud: "'Please be advised that the United States Senate formally requests that a representative of the Cheyenne Nation address the select committee on the subject of Indian education.' *Indian education!*"

Doreen added, "Alan Rowland wants Ted to represent the Cheyenne."

Leland's mind was going into overdrive. "Wow! What timing."

Ted reached for the telegram. "Let me see that."

Leland handed Ted the telegram. He took a moment reading it. Then Ted looked over to the BIA building and the American flag. "Maybe someone is ready to listen."

CHAPTER 19

THE LIGHT OF DAY

The building that houses the Department of the Interior in Washington, D.C., is impressive, as are all the structures that set forth the presence and scale of the United States government. Throughout Ted's years in the service and after, he had never been to the country's capitol until this trip.

Ted and Leland, both in suits and ties, sat on one side of a long table. On the other side were Dorothy, Tucker, the Director of the BIA's department on Indian education, and four men who were department associates.

Ted had been addressing the room, giving his concept of how the change to the current school system would work.

" . . . And we hope to create a, call it a teacher's workshop. The Tribal Council will introduce teachers to our cultural heritage, so programs and techniques for instructing our children will be consistent with what they have learned in our homes. Our history is rich and very old. The grandmothers speak with this knowledge of our ancient traditions."

The director was a pompous sort who was less than pleased to be spending an afternoon listening to the ideas of some less than important Indian from Montana. "We understand that you minority groups, through your *obstructionist*

practices, are promoting self-determination, your cause for
'civil liberties.' While you wish to preserve your individual cultures, we, at the Bureau of Indian Affairs, have the primary task
to provide a basic education to the now four hundred thousand Indian students that go to our Bureau-run schools."

Ted took a thoughtful moment before responding. "You
mentioned obstructionist practices? Would that include the
time I spent in the Army, fighting in Korea?"

The director cleared his throat. "I was speaking in gener-
alities. I am sure you understand."

"Perhaps more than you realize." Ted returned to the passion he felt for the subject that brought him there. "In today's
world, we have a lot of single mothers. It's probably that
way everywhere. They don't have time to listen to their kids.
They're too busy looking for ways to stay alive. So it's the
grandmothers. . . . "

The director could listen no more. He cut Ted off. "I say
to you, the dropout rate for Indian students is the highest in
the nation. So let me put this in terms I hope you comprehend. Perhaps you should be looking to hold the parents to
task for the lack of student interest, rather than attempting to
blame hard-working teachers and this agency for the student
failures."

This attitude was beginning to gnaw at Ted's insides. He
decided to shift gears. "Let me put this in terms that *you* can
understand. Our schools are on the verge of becoming shan-
tytowns. They are underfunded on every budgetary level. The
faculties do not meet the Department of Education standards.
They do not even meet your department's substandard levels."

The director, totally disinterested in continuing, looked at his watch. Ted reached for one more thought. "Answer this, please. How would you feel if the Nazis won the war and you were all forced to speak German, right here in Washington? If your new leaders were telling you that you can't speak English, that you can't use your own name, it must be German, how would you feel if your culture was not allowed to continue, if you were told that you had no right to do anything without German approval?"

The director was now getting very unsettled with this dialog.

Ted answered the question. "Bet you'd resist. In fact, you might have another tea party in Boston Harbor. Except you'd be dumping German beer."

The director got up. "The fact of the matter is, we won that war. And I have no more time for this. Miss Deville and Mr. Tucker may wish to continue, that's up to them."

The director looked over to his people. It was clear they wanted to end the meeting as well.

Dorothy picked up the lead from the director. "If there's more, perhaps we should pick it up tomorrow?"

Ted finished, "I've had my say. Mr. Pond will join you. Thanks for your time."

Ted exited the room. After a moment of surprise, Leland ran after him.

The director straightened his papers, then looked at his people. "Well, I think that went quite well."

No one responded.

He continued. "We can't lose. If the Senate presses us to do what the Indians want, and the Indians succeed, we'll be heroes for sponsoring them. And if the Indians fail, well, we were closing Busby anyway, and it will be their doing, their failure, not ours."

Ted was entering an elevator just as Leland rounded the corner. He called out, "Ted. Wait."

Leland just made it before the door closed.

Ted was in a space Leland had never seen from this positive force of a man.

Ted spoke without looking at his friend. "Attitudes of supremacy. I can't speak with those people. They care nothing for truth. The words, the hope, the vision of the future, it means nothing. Pointless."

Leland offered what he really believed would be a starting ground. "Well tomorrow, the Senate. It'll be different than this."

Ted shrugged it off. "You know what, Leland? If I don't show up, you testify on behalf of the Cheyenne. You're more than qualified, and you're educated. Maybe they'll listen to you."

The elevator door opened and Ted stepped into the crowd, leaving the building. Leland watched as Ted walked off. Perhaps for the first time he could remember, he was speechless.

Leland called Doreen from his hotel room later that afternoon. He described the tenor of the meeting. It was a disappointment for her to hear the kind of attitude they had run into, even though all too familiar. He told her about Ted's reaction and she became quiet.

Leland asked her to tell him about Ted. She danced around the main concern but finally confided about Ted's earlier life. She explained that he had been near death from alcohol poisoning years ago. She had never known him then and really only knew of his personal history because of his work with Vietnam vets, recovering alcoholics, and the lost souls trying to reenter domestic life after fighting in a war. Ted had told her his story, why it was he had come to work so hard for the tribe. Leland agreed that she should call Imogene and let her know what was going on.

At about that same time, Ted had stepped into an old-style, wooden phone booth sitting in the back corner of a tavern, the kind you can still see in the popular restaurants and bars built back in the earlier part of the twentieth century. Since this one looked out towards the tavern's bar, from his vantage point, Ted could see the bartender and the one patron. They were locked in what struck Ted as an innocuous discussion about the NFL.

Ted was desperate, feeling short of breath, as he dialed Imogene. When she answered, he launched into his concern. "Maybe after all this, the old man was right. Talking to these people is pointless."

"Hello to you, too."

"What do I do?"

Imogene showed no sympathy. "You've gone all the way to Washington, and that's what you ask me? Come home, Ted, and go over to Busby School. Try asking the kids. I don't want to hear it."

Ted was feeling claustrophobic. He loosened his collar and tie. "Imogene, you don't understand. You come here and try doing this."

"Ted, you wanted to rock the boat. Well, you have. And it's stormy. But you call me and tell me you're ready to jump overboard. I'm not going to listen to that shit. Not from you."

"Imogene, please don't say that."

"I'm tellin' you what I think. What did you want me to say?" Then in a sarcastic tone, she continued. "Oh, gee honey, you're right. I know things are tough. Come on home and I'll fix you a nice dinner."

Ted very carefully hung up the phone. He looked out of the booth toward the bar. After a moment, he slowly opened the door and walked in that direction.

He stood for a moment, looking on. All that dark wood, the warm-looking bottles of so many different varieties. The shiny glasses, the mirrors, the old brass light fixtures hanging over the bar, the leather-covered stools, and the brass foot rail. No wonder a downtown tavern felt so comfortable.

The bartender noticed Ted. "Hey, buddy, what'll it be?"

Ted's face was blank. The moment the question was asked, his mouth got wet inside from the thought of the taste of the bourbon. He took the three steps to the bar, pulled out a stool, and sat. He looked at the bartender for another moment and then said, "Bourbon and branch water."

"Check." The bartender was in his mid-fifties. Work in a bar long enough and you will see every type of drinker. He probably knew that Ted was an alcoholic, or so Ted assumed. The bartender put the glass in front of Ted. "Two-fifty."

Ted reached in his pocket and peeled off three dollars. He handed the bills to the bartender. "Keep the change."

"Check." Then he went back to polishing the glasses and his conversation with the other patron.

Ted pulled out the Zippo and lit a Camel. He still had the same lighter. Its casing was now mostly bronze, the plating having worn off over the years. The army emblem, too, was smoothly worn. Ted opened and closed it a few times. The feel of it still reassured him. They had covered a lot of the world together, he thought.

Ted took a long look at the drink sitting in front of him. Sweat was beginning to build on the glass. An image flashed through his thoughts of his days in the service, of getting totally blitzed in the non-coms bar on the base and staggering out the door, trying to find his way back to his quarters. Those days were so long ago it seemed to be a different lifetime. He had survived the South Pacific and Korea. He had survived his days with Helen. Then he had survived the lost years in Denver. He had finally done right by his daughters. He had put in years working for improvements with the Tribal Council. And here he was in Washington, D.C., arguing with people who had no idea what the Busby School meant to the children and parents of Lame Deer, Montana. The school and the students were just numbers, a part of some budget that was part of some appropriation that made up a part of some department that was part of some branch of government that was supposed to serve the people.

Ted was trying to understand how anything good was ever accomplished through this system of government. To be a bureaucrat, what kind of person would that be? Where do they come from? What qualifies them to hold so much responsibility for so many people?

The drink was just sitting there. Ted had smoked his second cigarette when he looked up, straight ahead, and caught his reflection in the mirror backing the bar. His image was hidden between bottles, but he was making eye contact. There he was, Ted Rising Sun, the great-grandson of Morning Star, his revered ancestor who had so much vision and strength, whose blood was part of what made Ted a decorated war hero. Here he sat, trying to put some meaning to life while staring down a glass of booze.

Ted pushed away from the drink and the bar, and walked out of the tavern, back into the light of day.

CHAPTER 20

ADAPTING TO SURVIVE

The National Mall, certainly a part of what George Washington had commissioned Pierre L'Enfant to plan as a center point to the city that was to be the capitol of the country, had become the site for national expressions of remembrance, observance and, as democracy would provide, protest.

For Ted, this revered place was now a point of contemplation. He walked in the shadow of the Washington monument, looking up to its 555-foot peak, down its obelisk design, and took in the sight of the fifty state flags that surrounded its base. The U.S. Cavalry was fighting a war with the Cheyenne and other Indian Nations during the time of the monument's construction.

How odd it was for Ted to be within view of such a symbol of the union and feel the influence of its purpose, while possessing the feelings that had erupted in his gut earlier in the Department of the Interior. Ted had served that union as a member of the Armed Forces. Yet, on the streets of Denver, he was just another Indian that belonged back on the reservation. And here, hours before, he was a mark on someone's calendar of appointments for the day, a gratuitous conference.

The Cheyenne were remote outcasts, a tiny segment of a massive population. The Indians of the country were so far removed from the mainstream, yet they had to be dealt with. The issue of "Civil Rights" was becoming a very popular building block for many a politician. But what did a cause that might build a career have to do with the essence of this great democratic society to which Ted belonged?

As Ted negotiated his way through the tourists, he happened on a group of placard-carrying Hippies protesting the war in Vietnam. They were dressed in fatigues, with bandanas tied around their heads. The men had hair as long as the women with them.

Later, alone with his thoughts, Ted walked around the thirty-six Doric columns that surround the sculpture of Abraham Lincoln. He studied the mural painted by Jules Guerin that depicts the angel of truth freeing a slave. What truth is there in this for the Indian? he wondered. What should this mean to the sixth grade class at Busby School? Then he stood at the top of the monument's stairs, looking across the mall. What did all of this have to do with the people like Tucker, Dorothy Deville, or the BIA director he met with earlier? The wonderful idea, the principle of freeing mankind from slavery, the core idea behind all that was symbolized by this national monument, was being strangled by the people who were supposed to serve the country.

Walking in the shade of the trees that line the edge of the mall, Ted was enjoying how things looked in the late afternoon light. He glanced back at the powerful sight of the Lincoln Memorial. Then he looked at the visitors who passed by, their cameras snapping pictures. Something struck him. These people were not just white. There were faces of every culture and nationality passing him by. These people were not drawn here because of the exquisite architecture but by the belief and dream that all of this represented to the world. Ultimately, those principles of freedom had been his purpose in the two wars in which he had risked his life. Then it struck him: Ted Rising Sun was a part of what all this stood for.

Ted took a seat on a bench near the street. He was lost in his thoughts when the flutter and pecking of a bird caught his attention. Ted saw a sparrow busily pecking at its reflection in the chrome on the front grill of an automobile parked nearby.

Ted was amused as he realized the bird was fighting with itself. "Can't win fighting yourself, little buddy." Just as he said that he realized how sweetly simple but how powerfully true that was. The sparrow seemed to look at him. Then Ted added, "I have learned that the hard way, believe me."

The bird began picking at the bugs collected on the front of the vehicle. Ted watched, pondered, and was amazed at how hard that bird was willing to work for food. His expression began to turn to admiration.

"Never give up, do you."

Once again the bird seemed to look at Ted. Then it continued with the harvest. Ted was struck by the thought that this creature of God, of *Maheo,* had once owned this land as much as the Cheyenne or anyone else. There had been no cars, no roads, no bulldozers to take down trees. But as man came and the land was populated with buildings, towns, cities, and considerably altered to accommodate all of that progress, this little bird had adapted. It had not given up to the changing world nor did it find an excuse in the need for new methods it would have to invent to find a meal. The sparrow adapted.

Ted remembered Grandmother's telling him about the sparrow she had watched with her father on a cold morning on the desperate trek home from the Indian Territories, how the wise old man had explained to his daughter that the little bird never gave up. It was a sparrow from the same family that Ted was now watching—a common little bird that had asserted itself in spite of predators, nature, and a changing habitat consisting mostly of concrete and asphalt.

At work right in front of Ted was one of nature's great examples. The sparrow illustrated that the nobility of the common person is undeniable. And there, sitting in the splendor of a warm afternoon, looking out at a sight that had inspired so many, Ted found inspiration from a tiny winged creature as a new sense of dignity overcame him.

"Makin' me feel pretty small right about now," he said to the bird. After a few moments Ted looked out at the blue sky.

"You were right. Someday, they will want to know, Grandmother."

Ted looked back at the bird. It took a last look at Ted and then suddenly flew away.

The Senate chamber was packed. The Indian Education Committee members were taking their seats. Ted Kennedy was the chairman. Many Indian Nations were represented.

From the front row, Leland was handing a Senate aide a stack of briefs. Ted entered the room and found his way to Leland. As he sat, Ted gave Leland a confident pat on the hand. Leland was extremely relieved, asking, "You okay?"

Ted assured him. "I'm great. Every meal's a feast, every day's a holiday."

Leland raised his eyebrows at the change, then smiled. "Good. It's you. You're back."

"Just wanted to take a little walk. Lots to see in this town, you know."

Senator Kennedy turned on his microphone and began the hearing. "Distinguished colleagues, honorable guests, ladies and gentlemen. Today we are commencing hearings that pertain to the conditions of the educational program now administered by the Bureau of Indian Affairs for the Department of the Interior. Before we begin, I would like to thank all those who have joined us from across this nation. I also wish to acknowledge my brother, Robert Kennedy, whose concern it was that all citizens of this great land have the opportunities afforded them by our constitution."

Kennedy went on for about ten minutes, which was followed by a few more introductory, politically-inspired speeches of goodwill. Following that, the testimony began.

Statement after statement delivered by members of the many Indian Nations of this country told of the same kind of conditions.

Then, after an hour and a half break for lunch, the testimony continued. Ted was first up for the afternoon session. He was seated at the center table, Leland at his side.

Ted leaned forward and pulled the table microphone close. He had no prepared speech on paper, no notes. He confidently began. His dark eyes, magnified by his glasses, made contact with each member of the committee as he spoke. "Chairman Kennedy, distinguished members of the Senate Committee on Indian Affairs, thank you for this invitation to speak before you on behalf of the Northern Cheyenne. My name is Ted Rising Sun. My Cheyenne name, given to me at birth, is High Hawk. I am proud of that name. It's engraved on my cigarette lighter, right under the U.S. Army's emblem."

Ted took the lighter out of his pocket and admired it for a moment before continuing. "I served this country in Korea as a member of the Twenty-fourth Infantry." He then returned it to his pocket.

"In the long history of the ancestors of all Indian Nations and the United States, you may not realize that eight hundred treaties have been negotiated. The Indian Nations, as a part of this treaty process, turned over *four hundred and fifty million acres of land*, with the clear promise that health care, education, housing, and other types of essentials would be provided by our new government, since the precious land we gave up was what had sustained our lifestyle for so many hundreds of years before.

"We were a people who knew nothing of cities. We had been hunters and gatherers throughout our entire existence. When the promise was made to us that if we would lay down our arms and relinquish our land, all our needs would be taken care of, our great Chief, Morning Star, believed and accepted this as truth. He believed that our children would go to schools and become educated in the white man's ways so they could live a good life in the changing world. Prior to this, our children were taught by the wisest members of the tribe, the grandmothers. They were taught through mentors and learned skills through the actual process of doing."

Each of the senators was truly listening to Ted, absorbed with his words.

Ted continued. "Since the beginning of the reservation system, the education of the Indian has been under the jurisdiction of the Bureau of Indian Affairs. Despite the specifics of the many treaties confirmed by the Supreme Court, in which the Indian Nations have inherent sovereignty over their members and their territories, we are not allowed to participate in the education of our children, even though this has been our desire. Yesterday, I was called an *obstructionist.* This happened because I want to speak to Washington officials about change.

"We believe the systematic training of teachers, taking into account the social and cultural process that had been established for hundreds of years with our people, is absolutely necessary. Morning Star, known as Dull Knife by many of you, traveled here a century ago and met with President Grant. Morning Star came away with great resolve and told the Cheyenne people, 'We should ask for schools. We can no longer live as we used to. We must learn this new way of life.'

"When I was eight-years-old, I asked my mother if I could go to school. I had avoided the police on the reservation up 'til that time. Their primary job was to enforce school attendance. Why did I ask to go to school, you might wonder? A friend of mine, like me, avoided school. He was caught by the police and his father attempted to intercede. His father was shot in the leg by the police while arguing for his son. At eight, I actually thought my dad would be shot if I did not go to school." Ted took a dramatic pause while he poured a small amount of water from a pitcher on the table. He took a sip while all eyes in the chamber watched.

"Going to school meant going away from home. We were only allowed to see our parents between one and five PM on each Saturday. We were not allowed to speak in Cheyenne, even though that was the language we had grown up with. If we were late returning from a family visit, even by five minutes, we were denied our dinner. And in that case, we also forfeited the next week's visit with our parents.

"This practice was abandoned and we are thankful. Today, if you wish to look at academic success, you must realize that American Indian students rank at the lowest level of every educational indicator, in primary, secondary, and college levels. The recent Census reports that forty-three percent of American Indian children live in poverty. Unemployment on some of the larger reservations is several times higher than national levels. Without education, our people have no chance of seeing these conditions improve.

"Distinguished Senators, help us help ourselves. We want to open the door to education. Our children will learn. Give them the opportunity, please. Let us be involved with our children's future."

Ted pushed the microphone back and leaned into the chair. A warm smile came over his face and all he could think of was Grandmother, sitting in the room and listening. She was there, most certainly, and her prophecy was being fulfilled in that moment. These men did listen. They did want to know.

At the days end, while those remaining were moving through the crowded corridor, Ted and Leland stepped from the chamber. A PBS television journalist rushed to them. "Mr. Rising Sun and Mr. Pond, would you take a moment to be interviewed?"

Ted replied with no hesitation. "Sure."

Leland immediately straightened his tie. They followed the journalist towards an alcove where a cameraman was waiting. The journalist, a woman in her mid-twenties, was showing real excitement with the day's testimony. "I think they'll do something to change things for your people, Mr. Rising Sun."

Ted was all smiles. "That would be great."

She continued. "The word we got is that Kennedy was very impressed with your address to the committee. In fact, I heard one of the Senators say 'You pack some powerful medicine.'"

Leland laughed, "He sure does that."

Ted chuckled and a devilish feeling overcame him. "You know, my grandfather taught me to always make my medicine around something really powerful. He made his medicine around his horses."

The journalist started taking notes, expecting a great and wise Indian lesson in this.

Ted continued. "I make my medicine around education. That's the power of the future."

She smiled.

Ted then added, "But, if my grandfather were alive today, he'd make his medicine around the two hundred and fifty horses under the hood of his Ford pickup."

The journalist broke out in laughter. "You know, Mr. Rising Sun, you could work in this town."

Ted got a sly grin. "I am."

They laughed again before settling into the interview.

CHAPTER 21
A NEW DAY AT BUSBY

A student was raising the American flag. Ted, Imogene, Ruthie and Myra (now in their early twenties), Leland and Doreen, were accompanied by the members of the Tribal Council. The new school principal, a woman in her mid-forties, along with other teachers and students, were also attending this simple opening day ceremony. A local newspaper photographer was taking pictures.

With the flag raising over, Ted posed with the principal for a press shot. She had a very nice smile, an important complement to her position as the new leader of this school.

The principal turned to Ted. "Congratulations. Quite a day in history, this being the first Indian run school in this country. I'm feeling a little overwhelmed."

"Don't. You're going to do fine."

"Thank you for your trust, Mr. Rising Sun."

"I would prefer it if you called me Ted."

At that point the photographer snapped the picture. As the principal turned to speak with a reporter, Ted motioned to Ruthie, Myra, and Imogene to join him. Then he turned to the photographer and asked, "Take one of my family, will you?"

"No problem. Be glad to."

The family grouped up. Ted put his arm around Imogene.

She did the same, then looked up at him with a proud smile.

Ted leaned down close to her. "Thanks, babe. Never would of pulled this off without you."

She gave him a wink. "Whatta you doing later, soldier?"

Ted grinned. "Got any ideas?"

Joe Smith stepped in to congratulate Ted, as did Leland. Doreen joined them also.

"Well Ted, what's next?"

He pondered the question for a moment. "Let's start our own college."

Joe Smith quickly approved. "Great idea!"

Myra, Ruthie, and Doreen nodded in approval, but Leland feigned angst.

Ted was looking across the street from the school at a vacant lot. "We'll build it right over there!"

Leland looked and then turned to Ted. "You know, I just might be able to negotiate a really good deal for that land."

"Pro bono, of course," Ted said.

EPILOGUE

As one of the charter members of the board of the Indian Action Program, Ted Rising Sun would indeed see the opening of the Dull Knife Memorial College in 1975. The college, named in honor of one of the Northern Cheyenne's most respected leaders, Morning Star, answered to his prophetic words in which he looked to the education of the children as the future of the Cheyenne people.

The college started in a single facility at Lame Deer, consisting of one large building with six classrooms, four shop areas, and three rooms for offices. The college earned accreditation in 1977 as a two-year community college. Indians desiring an undergraduate education could then receive it on the reservation without driving 100 miles to attend college.

Ted saw the college expand to include additional classrooms and office space, a cafeteria, a large auditorium, and a library.

In October of 1991, Ted Rising Sun was named National Indian Elder of the Year, which came at a time when he was fighting diabetes, had lost some of his toes to the illness, and was barely able to cover the expense of living.

The award was presented to him by the National Indian Education Association in Omaha, Nebraska. Doreen Pond and others helped raise the money for Ted to travel from Lame Deer to Omaha. There, more than 2,000 Indian educators from across the United States stood to honor Ted's tireless dedication to the improvement of Indian education. As a direct result of Ted's and others' extraordinary efforts, Congress passed the Indian Self-Determination Act in 1975. Today, over fifty-six community-controlled schools operate under contract with the BIA, modeled after the first contract school in Busby, Montana.

Ted was so emotionally seized by the recognition at the conference ceremony, he was barely able to speak when presented the award. This homage had come after so many years with little recognition for his taxing work. While this great honor acknowledged what had been his adult calling, it was also remembered that Ted had served his country in service to the military during both WWII in the Pacific and then during the Korean War when he voluntarily reenlisted.

In these later years, Ted had an enormous advantage that he applied to his endeavors as part of the Tribal Council. He had learned through his own painful life that while being a moderating voice, he could win the battles with his spoken words, concepts, and values. Much as Oliver had taught him patience as a child, Ted ascertained a wisdom about life through his mentor's lessons and his life experiences.

Ultimately, Ted lost both his legs to diabetes. They were amputated at the VA hospital in Sheridan, Wyoming. When his grandchildren came to visit him at the hospital, Ted played with them about how he lost his legs, turning his painful situation into a little game that told the kids their grandpa was still okay. He would give the kids rides on his lap from his wheelchair. They loved their grandfather.

After Ted's death, his grandchildren have gone to see his grave and decorate it on days of remembrance. They ask their mothers or Imogene, "Did Grandpa go to heaven?"

"Yes, he's in heaven."

Ted Rising Sun was sixty-eight when he passed away on April 5, 1995.

The Sand Creek massacre took the lives of 109 Cheyenne and Arapaho women and children, and twenty-eight of their men, who had been guaranteed safety by representatives of the United States. The Colorado Historical Society, the Colorado National American Heritage Council, and the Colorado Department of Highways, through an endowment, erected a commemorative marker at Chivington, Colorado, in 1986 that reads:

Sand Creek Massacre: November 29, 1864 was an unforgettable day for the Cheyenne and Arapaho. On the banks of Sand Creek stood a camp of about 100 Cheyenne and some ten Arapaho lodges established, by what may have been taken as the order of the U.S. Army Commander at the nearby Fort Lyon . . . Black Kettle, a leader and spokesman for the camp, hoisted an American flag to convey that the camp was peaceful. Ignoring the signal, volunteer militia, led by Colonel John M. Chivington, attacked killing all in their path. With many of the men away, organized resistance was impossible . . . More than 137 Indian people, mostly women and children, lay dead, their bodies mutilated. The brutal attack was denounced in congressional hearings, but none of the participants was punished.

The breakout and massacre at Fort Robinson took the lives of sixty-four Cheyenne. Most of these were women and children. Fort Robinson is now an historical site. The Nebraska Historical Society has established markers at the fort, which tell of the outbreak. The land once occupied by the cavalry barracks that the Cheyenne were imprisoned in, and broke free from, is staked to show the size of the building. At its side the original adjutant's office, built from logs, stands as it did in 1878.

Of the 12,000 Indian children required to attend Carlisle Indian School during its thirty-nine years, only 758 graduated. In this regard, Ted Rising Sun had explained:

"The U.S. government decided the best approach to *civilizing* the Indians was to make us like the white man, and the best way to accomplish this was through education.

"At six years of age every Cheyenne child was expected in school, many of which were boarding schools far from their homes. If the children did not go to school, then the family did not get its rations. The Cheyenne had nothing to say about how the school was run, what would be taught there, who would do the teaching. All this was decided by the Bureau of Indian Affairs."

Little Wolf and his followers had been found in the northern country by White Hat Clark and brought back to Red

Cloud. When the government relented and allowed the Cheyenne their land, Morning Star, Little Wolf, and the others lived in the Rosebud Valley. Little Wolf's death came in 1904 of natural causes. Morning Star died in 1883. He had survived the wars, the trek south, and finally had led his people to their home in the Tongue River Reservation.

It is fitting that Liberty is represented by a woman, as does the blindfolded lady represent justice. But most befitting is that to each of us, this sphere of life we are given, spun by the planet on which we reside, is known to so many cultures as mother earth. She provides life to all as does Lady Liberty provide the symbol and belief of freedom to the people who live within her shores.

The Lady just stands
Out there in the harbor
on her plinth
With her right hand
extended high over her head
Holding her torch
Of Sweet Liberty
While in her left hand,
Frederick Auguste Bertholdi, scupltor
put a book of law.

Inscribed within:

July 4, 1776
The land of the free
and the home of the brave.
Who will keep her standing
with her torch held high
for freedom is a precious thing
never easily attained
and never easily kept
Often taken for granted
until we are reminded
by the Lady with her torch
greeting us in New York Bay.

APPENDIX

THE CONGRESSIONAL ACT
Public Law 105-243
105th Congress

An Act: To authorize the Secretary of the Interior to study the suitability and feasibility Oct. 6, 1998 of designating the Sand Creek Massacre National Historic Site in the State (S.1695) of Colorado as a unit of the National Park System, and for other purposes.

Be it enacted by the Senate and House of Representatives of the United States of America in Congress assembled,

SECTION 1.
SHORT TITLE Sand Creek Massacre

This Act may be cited as the "Sand Creek Massacre National Historic Site Study Act of 1998."

SEC. 2. FINDINGS

(a) FINDINGS. —Congress finds that—

(1) on November 29, 1864, Colonel John M. Chivington led a group of 700 armed soldiers to a peaceful Cheyenne village of more than 100 lodges on the Big Sandy, also known as Sand Creek, located within the Territory of Colorado and in a running fight that ranged several miles upstream along the Big Sandy, slaughtered several hundred Indians in Chief Black Kettle's village, the majority of whom were women and children;

(2) the incident was quickly recognized as a national disgrace and investigated and condemned by two congressional committees and a military commission;

(3) although the United States admitted guilt and reparations were provided for in Article VI of the Treaty of the Little Arapaho Tribe, Arkansas, of October 14, 1865 (14 Stat. 703) between the United States and the Cheyenne and Arapaho Tribes of Indians, those treaty obligations remain unfulfilled;

(4) land at or near the site of the Sand Creek Massacre may be available for purchase from a willing seller; and

(5) the site is of great significance to the Cheyenne and Arapaho Indian descendants of those who lost their lives at the incident at Sand Creek and to their tribes, and those descendants and tribes deserve the right of open access to visit the site and rights of cultural and historical observance at the site.

BIBLIOGRAPHY

1. Proceedings of a Board of Officers, convened by virtue of the special order of the Department of the Army. Fort Robinson, NE, January 25, 1879. Testimony of the witnesses to the Cheyenne Outbreak.

2. Oral History of the Cheyenne Indians, Ted Rising Sun, recorded in audio on March 28, 1983, Busby, Montana.

3. Don Hollow Breast, various writings of historical stories of the Cheyenne.

4. Oral History of Northern Cheyenne, Art McDonald, Doreen "Walking Woman" Pond, by John Kuri, 9/24/00, 9/25/00, 9/26/00, 9/27/00, 10/23/00.

5. Oral History of Northern Cheyenne, Art McDonald, by John Kuri, 9/23/00, 10/19/00, 10/20/00, 10/21/00, 10/22/00.

6. J. Douglas McDonald, A. L. McDonald, Bill Tall Bull, & Ted Rising Sun, *The "Cheyenne Outbreak" Revisited*, Another Look at the Most Significant Night in the History of the Northern Cheyenne People, 1987, 3–7.

7. Audio/Video tape transcription of Ted Rising Sun with Art McDonald, Tapes 1, 2, part of 3.

8. Audio/Video tape transcription of Bill Tall Bull with Art McDonald, Tapes 3–7.

9. Oral History, Imogene Rising Sun, by John Kuri, 10/20/00. (Widow of Ted Rising Sun)

10. Ray Allen Billington, Martin Ridge, *Westward Expansion,* 5th Edition, (New York: MacMillan Publishing Co., 1982), 606. (Billington, Late of the Huntington Library and Art Gallery; Ridge, Senior Research Associate, Huntington.)

11. Howard Fast, *The Last Frontier,* (New York: Duell, Sloan and Pearce, 1941), 11–13, 26, 33, 94–111, 131–133, 163–165, 181–190, 206–211, 213–307.

12. Dee Brown, *Bury My Heart at Wounded Knee,* (New York: Bolt, Rinehart, & Winston, 1970), 9–10, 67–102, 310–313, 331–349, 333–338, 415–438, 427.

13. Rubie Sooktis, Vern Sooktis, *Trek North,* Big Sky Video 1996, (includes interviews with Ted Rising Sun and tour of Fort Robinson breakout site).

14. Doreen "Walking Woman" Pond, Arthur L. McDonald, *Cheyenne Journey,* (Santa Ana: Seven Locks Press, 1996), 6, 9, 10, 20–24, 27, 28, 35, 36, 41–48, 50, 53, 54, 58, 61, 62, 64, 66, 71, 72, 77, 80, 83, 84, 89–91, 100, 105, 116, 119, 120, 124.

15. Mari Sandoz, *Cheyenne Autumn,* (New York: McGraw-Hill, 1953), v–vii, xv–xx, 1–11, 14–23, 25–27, 30–33, 35–39, 41,

45, 47–50, 53–56, 59, 62–66, 70–85, 87, 89–92, 94v100, 104, 106–111, 113–137, 139–141, 143, 146, 147, 150, 151, 154, 156, 157,166–178, 180–195, 197–210, 212, 213, 216–219, 222–237, 240–244, 246, 248–250, 252, 253, 255, 256, 258–260, 262–268, 271.

16. Jean Afton, David Fridtjof Halaas, & Andrew E. Masich, with Richard N. Ellis, *Cheyenne Dog Soldiers, A Ledgerbook History of Coups and Combat,* (Niwot: University Press of Colorado, 1997), xiii–xviii, xxviii, xxix, xxx, xxxii, 11, 15, 39–43, 63, 76, 77, 83, 88, 89, 101, 107, 132, 141, 156, 167, 259–261, 323.

17. Charles Phillips, *Heritage of the West,* (Surrey, England, Colour Library Books Ltd., 1992), 108–111, 119–135.

18. Thomas R. Buecker, *Fort Robinson and the American West,* (Lincoln: Nebraska State Historical Society, 1999), 125–148, photo plates that follow page 148.

19. Greg McCracken, "Cheyenne Man Honored," *The Billings Gazette,* (November 15, 1991), p. 6-B.

The following regarding Indian Education, at Carlisle, Busby, and other reservation schools:

20. The ERIC Digests. ED314228, Jon Reyhner, 1989. Changes in American Indian Education: A Historical Retrospective.

21. Testimony before the Senate Committee on Indian Affairs.

a. Tribal Sovereignty.

b. Indian Elementary and Secondary Education Authorization.

c. National Indian Health Board Report

d. Testimony on Senate Bill 1658.

22. National Education Association Brief to the NEA and the NEIA on American Indian Education.

23. Paula Gunn Allen (Laguna Sioux), editor, *Voice of the Turtle: American Indian Literature 1900–1970,* Random House, 1994, 111–112, 116–117.

24. George E. Hyde, *Spotted Tail's Folk: A History of the Brul Sioux,* (Norman: University of Oklahoma, 1989), 278, 289, 292–293.

25. LaVera Rose (Lakota), *Grandchildren of the Lakota,* (Lerner, 1999).

26. Genevieve Bell, *Telling Stories Out of School: Remembering the Carlisle Indian Industrial School, 1879–1918,* Ph.D. Thesis, Stanford University, 1998.

27. Alvin Josephy, *500 Nations,* (Alfred A. Knopf, 1994), 432, 434.

28. Brenda J. Child (Ojibwe), *Boarding School Seasons: American Indian Families, 1900–1940,* (Lincoln: University of Nebraska, 1998) 13.

29. Peter Nabokow, *Native American Testimony,* (Viking 1978, revised 1991) Lone Wolf (Blackfoot) oral history, 220.

The following Historical Museums and Historical Sites have been visited:

30. Fort Robinson, Nebraska.

31. Sand Hills adjacent to Fort Robinson, Nebraska. (Escape route) Subject of paper, *The"Cheyenne Outbreak" Revisited*, # 6 above.

32. Bordeaux Trading Post & Museum, Chadron, Nebraska.

33. Tongue River Reservation.

34. Wind River Reservation.

The following is a quote from Post Surgeon E.B. Mosley, in the aftermath of the Cheyenne Breakout, that is inscribed at the fort museum.

"During this whole period the fighting was of the most desperate character being from hand to hand struggle up to a range of almost always inside fifty yards. The great proportion of fatal wounds is remarkable and the concentration on the trunk of the body shows a deliberation and skill in handling the improved breech loading arms, a feat which explains why this particular tribe enjoyed the reputation of being the best warriors on the plains."

The opening poem was written by James Pond, an enrolled member of the Northern Cheyenne Nation. He holds two Masters Degrees, one in microbiology, one in medical technology, and is currently the head of the laboratory for Indian Health Services, Lapwai, Idaho.